Single and Loathing It

A Novel

Michael Dennis

Single and Loathing It

"don't take up comedy."

—ex-girlfriend

for mom & dad. i hope you never read this.

1

I met her ordering a drink at Bar Napoli, an upscale cocktail joint in the downtown Clayton Business District in St. Louis. She and her friend were drinking vodka-waters, which I think was to do with the low caloric content—unless of course they just enjoyed the burning taste of nail-polish remover. I decided to insert myself into whatever conversation they were having. Slyly leaning over, I utter, "All right gals, what are we talking about?" It is a pick-up line, but I disguised it as otherwise in the form of friendly banter and they took the bait.

"We're talking about how trashy those girls over there look." She said this with authentic vitriol, despite not knowing anything about the girls in question. A conjecture created out of thin, jealous air. The girls they were referring to were actually very attractive, angelic almost, but I knew how to rig my opinion to suit the direction of the conversation.

"Jesus, who let the swamp scum in?" I replied. Insulting their enemies on the other side of the bar amused them and they turned their full attention to me. I looped in my male counterpart Jim, because from experience one girl was typically more than enough for me to handle, both verbally and sexually. Two women at once? Who am I, fucking Russell Brand? Jim thankfully entertained one of the girls in conversation. After about 20 minutes of witless gibberish, I had one of their phone numbers. Her name was Lauren. Before leaving, I told her how nice it was to meet her and that I would text her *soon*.

After that chance encounter I waited 40 days and 40 nights before sending her a message. I did not want to come off as too eager. The three-day rule is complete and utter nonsense. Women are much too smart for that barbaric blueprint that male buffoons abide by. They know exactly what you're doing.

It was actually only two days later when I sent a text, maybe three, but I digress. I usually had a couple different approaches in my first text methodology depending on what I could remember of the girl's personality. In this instance, Lauren struck me as kind of an awful human being, so I went with: *I still can't get over those rancid girls at Napoli. LOL*

I hated acronyms like LOL, but she didn't know that. This was the invented affable version of myself that I used in an attempt to relate to women and with any luck entice them. She responded with enthusiasm and verve and the conversation evolved and flowed. I wasted no time and asked her out to dinner on Friday night. I soon realized that I had just made two concurrent mistakes.

Firstly I asked her out to dinner. I had known this girl for all of 20 minutes and three texts, how did I know she was worth food? Cuisine is expensive. You should not care about a girl's proper nourishment until at least the third date, like a true gentleman. It should have been a drinks-only invite. Mistake number two? I chose the wrong night of the week. Fridays are fun and there's a lot of social activity going on. Lauren had more of a Thursday vibe to her. I acknowledged my errors, but not until after she accepted. Real estate agents often call this 'buyer's remorse'.

Friday quickly arrived. Contrary to public opinion I was a halfway decent person, so I kept our first date plans intact. From the witless chatter I remembered she lived in Clayton, so I suggested the neighborhood staple, Tani Sushi Bistro for dinner. Choosing a restaurant near her was not for her convenience, it was for mine. Here's a quick intro lesson in theoretical probability. Statistically speaking, if the destination is close to where she lives she may just get an Uber or allow me to pick her up rather than drive herself. This will result in a higher probability of alcohol intake, thus resulting in a higher probability of having a fun time, which equates to a higher probability of having sex when I drop her home later. Worst-case scenario—hand stuff. Pay attention in math class, kids.

She opted for the Uber to meet me there, thank God. I drove a 2008 Chevy Cobalt. Cobalts do *not* exude sex in the eyes of a Clayton woman—or any woman for that matter. Sushi was an imperative on the first date because it signified that I was refined and cultured, I could use chopsticks, and I radiated sophistication. Truthfully, it is the perfect meal in the art of the first date. No embarrassingly sloppy mouthfuls, you can share food without causing nausea to other diners nearby, and it is light on the stomach but filling enough to give you increased energy for the pursuit of mediocre sex.

I arrived early and was seated at a half-booth-half-table-who-knows-what arrangement in the corner with a candle lit mid-table. Tani Sushi Bistro had a real match.com commercial atmosphere to it that somehow made everyone dining look more attractive. I ordered a Sapporo beer in honor of cultural appropriation and drank it while I glanced the restaurant over to make sure I didn't know anyone. Not because I was embarrassed to be seen with Lauren, I just hated most of the people I knew. As luck would have it I recognized no one. As I waited, I sat there and thought about my new client I was assigned earlier that day at my advertising firm. It was a sole proprietor business called Out da Trunk, which was actually just a guy selling used CDs out of the trunk of his car. He wanted me to help him market his crap better and he paid our fee in cash. It was a weird day at work. It was at that moment in Tani I realized he probably sold more than CDs.

I saw movement at the door and there she was. Astonishingly average looking. Not too bad. Just my type. Lauren's outfit and demeanor on this night demonstrated that she was probably the type of girl with hundreds of pointless Instagram selfies, all with the same oblique camera angle and come-hither facial expression paired with a completely irrelevant motivational quote.

I called her over as I flapped my hand above my head, waving, like a flamboyant psycho. This again was the feigned good guy version of myself, not the real Chris Van Zandt. In my 29-year-old history I had never waved my hand above my head in that manner before. It was a new and stupid gesture. As she approached, I slid her chair out for her with my foot while staying seated, like a casual gentleman.

"You look... pretty okay, I guess," I said, kind of joking. She was flattered. She ordered a vodka-water with lime again, her evident drink of choice. We wasted no time exploring the deeper waters of our personalities as she inquired about the profound subject of… *hobbies*. One of the most tedious conversation topics in the existence of first dates, just behind siblings and job titles. Her hobbies included a monotonous list of things that literally everyone does, including naps. Naps! One of her hobbies was falling asleep in the middle of the day. Quite quickly it turned out she had all the personality of a toaster and the sober conversation was difficult to grin and bear. She continued to speak but it fell on deaf ears. I swigged the rest of my beer in three gulps as I came to the realization that I would never see this girl again.

This is an unfortunate point in anyone's dating history. The stage of a date where you realize you never want to be seen in public with that person ever again. It is all too familiar. For me, a lot of different things happen during this phase. I stop caring. I start to say unsavory things. My drinking transforms from casual to methodical. I became less chivalrous and a bit lewder and a lot more vulgar. My main goal for the remainder of this particular date was to amuse myself.

Traditionally within this stage I was still trying to get laid, sure, but there was no future in it. No dating candidate could come back from this. Lauren was too far back in the rear-view and the mirror was smashed into hundreds of uninteresting pieces. She could have literally said, "Want to go back to my place and have sex? I live in a mansion with bumper cars and a Slamball court. My father is Mick Jagger and he bought it for me. You can invite your friends and other hot girls over. I also have *Road House* on my home cinema and a playful Golden Retriever named Ted," and I would have still incontrovertibly believed there was no future. Obviously, I would accept that offer and meet Ted, but overcoming that feeling of incompatibility on a first date is insurmountable. And I am not attempting to say that I was holier-than-thou by the way. More times than not the girl was the protagonist in this narrative and I was the undateable schmuck.

So I hadn't even ordered my Tani best-selling Cenzo Roll yet and all I could think about was how badly I wanted to leave. Everyone who has dated knows this feeling. In the movies or on TV they fake a phone call from their friend or neighbor and then say something terrible has happened. "Oh my gosh, that was my neighbor, Mrs. [mumble-something-resembling-a-last-name-here]. My apartment is on fire and I have to leave right now. I'm so sorry. I'll call you." But I was a trooper. I chose to carry on and get exponentially drunk instead. It made me enjoy her presence as much as one possibly could in the circumstances. And vice versa. I suggest that everyone in this dating scenario try it. If I was drunk enough, I probably could have talked to a group of plastic mannequins about tax returns and still enjoyed myself.

The date continued and my profanity and irreverence shifted back on the side of amatory charm and bon viveur nonchalance. She was loving my infantile sense of humor. She couldn't get enough of my 'that's what she said' witticism and toilet jokes. As she basked in the light of my true self, I realized she really was an awful person just as I had suspected.

After paying the bill, Lauren and I went home together and wrote drunken naked poetry only to never see each other again. Because at the end of the day, while us romantically oppressed singles are looking for love, it's okay to occasionally have slapdash sex with a borderline stranger for the sake of fun, even if you vehemently despise them as a human being. This was being single. And loathing it.

2

The reputation of a big city is often misconstrued by those who live outside of it. They haven't stepped foot there for years, but they will assuredly deem it uninhabitable. Crime rates and statistics. Economical data. Unfavorable news stories—all help to illustrate its urban disrepute. I was living in St. Louis, Missouri, for five brilliantly miserable years. Never stabbed. Never mugged. Never shot. Some people considered the city a hyper-segregated, crime-laden, racist cesspool of human filth that's too afraid or too poor to leave. Fair point, but I considered it home. No one from my past life understood the 'why' of it—why choose to stay in St. Louis? I was often asked this by old friends back in my small Wisconsin hometown for my reasoning. I rarely answered it earnestly and usually brushed it off with a joke. Something about conducting an anthropological study. Or loving the crime and the beggars, watching it all from my downtown loft window with binoculars while I ate fresh popcorn. I had a rotation of answers, all sarcastic. The truth is I moved to St. Louis years ago for my job. It was one of the few areas hiring in my field at the time. That's always the case with relocating. It's either for work or a lover. Nobody moves just to move.

Not to St. Louis anyways. Highest STD rate, third-highest crime rate, no NFL team, blatant racism, corrupt police, homelessness everywhere, pizzas made with the wrong cheese, and summers that were too long and too hot. The appeal was minimal.

But in reality, St. Louis suited me. The bars were cheap. The women were loose, I think. I don't know, I never really understood that term. Most importantly, outsiders like myself were intriguing to the locals. I was the adult equivalent of the new kid in class—the one who got kicked out of his old high school for pissing in lockers and wore a black leather jacket and whose mom got a job in the cafeteria to get his meal plan for free. It was a fresh identity in a stale city, but it was fitting.

I worked for an advertising firm downtown. An executive of sorts, my job was to create slogans and ad campaigns for clients—mostly start-ups or companies that wanted to rebrand. The work never seemed terribly monotonous; it was sometimes interesting, almost. I made it through the week just fine in eager anticipation of the weekend, much like a horny teenager tolerates the boring dialogue parts of *Basic Instinct*, yearning for the suggestive Sharon Stone scenes.

I lived in a large one-person loft several blocks down the street from my office on Washington Avenue. I loved everything about living downtown, even the vagrants and the panhandlers. Every day numerous bums would ask me for loose change or the more ambitious ones would suggest a few dollars. I would usually reply the same to all, "I was going to ask you the exact same thing." They never laughed. Homelessness and hopelessness flatten one's sense of humor I guess.

I was 29 years old and blatantly unhappily single. I

was not desperately single however; not a completely desolate unfuckable cretin. I was frequently meeting women and going on dates, occasionally bedding the 'loose' ones. But I never considered myself a womanizer, because aside from the occasional casual encounter, my intention with most of them was to find my life partner. I just happened to be very, very bad at the selection process. Deficient dating dexterity.

I had piercing blue eyes, medium-to-long, curly blond hair, and was relatively fit. I suppose you could say I was conventionally attractive, even despite the noticeable Woody Harrelson-like gap between my two front teeth. My parents always told me it was a tough financial decision not to get me braces when I was a kid. They explained how expensive they were and that I should love myself for the way God made me. I sort of understood... until they bought a hot tub and a new Prius for themselves two weeks after I moved out of the house aged 18.

Every morning on my walk to work down Washington Avenue I would count how many female strangers I saw that I wanted to have sex with. This appalling carnal exercise was purely a mental one to make the walk less boring. Never would I bother any of these women (or the lone gorgeous, long-haired, clean shaven man on June 14th of last year that I accidentally thought was a woman from a distance) other than by looking in their general direction. I was aware of its crassness. No one other than a co-worker knew of my daily ritual. The record was around 37 one Friday morning when there was a National Herbalife convention downtown. While I wanted to sleep with them, I also loathed and pitied them at the same time because they were dumb enough to fall into the mindless trap of the Ponzi scheme that is Herbalife. But they were attractive and desirable. Beautiful houses with nobody home. God's most noble creatures—Herbalife chicks.

So yeah, I was definitely a weird guy. I took the Rorschach test once, the one with the inkblots that are open to interpretation. All I saw were boobs and penises. I provocatively told the shrink who administered it that sanity was an imperfection and that he was more unstable than his patients. I lived a normal life for the most part, just with abnormal internal monologues. Despite a weird personality and overall demeanor, I was just eccentric and apathetic enough to be considered interesting to some women.

But yes, the women. There was always a powerful potency that came with meeting one. And every time I did, I assumed she was the one... at least for a few seconds. I became enamored and started daydreaming about our lives together, enjoying the limerence, but the odds were almost unequivocally that she was not in fact 'the one'. Upon realization of this I became uninterested, if not almost disgusted, as their flaws would begin to manifest in front of my eyes. But giving up on women was self-defeating. And wildly depressing. So I carried on. Bars, mutual friends, the occasional dating app—the resources were endless. I even picked up a girl at a vending machine once. She was buying Pop-Tarts.

3

The Sunday Scaries—a stupid millennial term describing the feeling you get as your Sunday evening turns into Sunday night and fills your mind and body with an unseemly feeling of dread and anxiety. Going to work the next morning after a booze-soaked 48 hours that leaves your central nervous system a corroded, irreparable wreck. I never truly experienced the Sunday Scaries, but I can describe it in explicit detail because every other whiny millennial on the face of the planet talked about it in agonizing detail. I never really disliked my job. Or it's possible that I was never engaged seriously enough to care. Either way, Monday mornings were never a complaint-worthy chore. If anything, I felt a sense of purpose. Somewhere I knew I was supposed to be. Things I knew I was supposed to accomplish. Our office was in a five-story renovated warehouse. Our owners thought they were very hip when they leased the entire third floor loft with exposed brick walls, high ceilings with wooden rafters, and wooden columns holding together the infrastructure throughout. They said things like 'collaborative' and 'open' when describing the layout of the place. No one had private offices—we all had 'workspaces' on a bench-style row of large laminate tables with vertical dividers too short to ignore your immediate neighbors. Needless to say I knew my colleagues quite well. To the right of me was Jill, an account manager. She was an odd combination of plain yet delightful, like a 9-grain oat slice of bread. She was never too intrusive and always thoughtful and respectful. It was for this reason we never shared a real relationship outside of the office walls. She was too nice for the likes of me. My social behavior beyond the company walls would have frightened her in no uncertain terms. She was the angel on my right shoulder Monday through Friday. Before I get to the devil on my left shoulder, let me first preface. Your relationships with your co-workers can be an interesting dynamic. You are compelled to interact with these people five days a week. You must get along with them relatively well. You might even meet your future wife, new best friend or possibly your archenemy all in the same relatively small space. I met arguably none of those three at my job, although not for lack of trying on the wife part. More on that later. Liking or disliking your co-workers, often a combination of the two, affects your everyday happiness. It also has a direct effect on the difficulty of your job as well. At our advertising firm, I had the pleasure and displeasure of meeting one of the most interesting yet peculiar people I've ever known. The devil on my left shoulder was named Greg. Greg was in his early thirties and sat next to me for several years. I cherished our conversations for the pure absurdity of them. His theories, thoughts, and comments were wildly unlike anything your average co-worker might come up with. A backstory on Greg is necessary to give some examples. Here are a few facts:

Greg had a son, Joseph, who was conceived out of

wedlock when he was just 19 years old.

His own father once fired him from his summer job after finding out that Greg called in sick to go to Six Flags with a friend.

Greg kept a portable mini-exercise bike underneath his desk that he bought on Craigslist for $25. He would operate it sporadically throughout the day urging everyone else in the office to find one and do the same because 'your health is all you have'.

Greg had spent thousands over the years on hair restorative products such as Propecia and different laser combs. The only time he wasn't wearing a baseball hat was when he was at work. Any other setting, he would usually be wearing what he called a 'CC' (Confidence Cap). His hairline was considered completely normal in every respect to anyone other than himself. Neuroticism was the culprit here.

Greg was what most people would call a hypochondriac. He often made appointments with doctors with very vague symptoms thinking he had AIDS. The doctor would ask what was wrong and he'd just say, "Something doesn't feel right, doc. I feel tired a lot."

Greg drove a 2010 Nissan Altima with neon underglow and always had the same Nickelback CD playing. He still lived at home with his parents at 33 years of age for no good reason whatsoever. He had been in this well-paying job for years. He once admitted to me that he had $67,000 in his savings account, just sitting there and slowly growing bigger with no real monthly expenses other than his son's youth hockey fees.

The first experience I had with Greg outside of the office was a Friday happy hour that turned into more of a late-night affair. Greg went around to strangers offering them a beer from one of our company-purchased beer buckets in exchange for a spare cigarette. One person he asked said, "I don't smoke, man." Greg looked him square in the eye and responded with, "It's not your fault, it's your parents' fault." I had no idea what it meant but the guy threatened to beat him up. Later that same night Greg tried to convince our team to go to a gay bar with him. Greg wasn't gay, at least not openly so, but he was obsessed with gay bars. He liked the treatment he received from other patrons, extracting a sense of self-confidence from their compliments. When he couldn't convince any of us to go, he went by himself.

Greg spent half the day doing actual work and the other half of the day trolling Facebook. He would write on the walls of people from his high school that he never talked to in person, comment flippantly on business pages, and messaged girls he knew of but also never spoke to in person. He typed comments like, 'thirsty' and 'too much makeup' on girls' photos simply to garner a reaction.

His son's mother and he had not been romantic in 12 years, but he did have an on-again off-again relationship with a girl named Julie, who he claimed to be the love of his life. It was the unhealthiest relationship I'd ever heard of. They broke up every couple months and would be separated for three or five weeks, then they would meet at some arbitrary place in public like the zoo or museum to go over 'bullet points'. These included some of the most abnormal and anomalous relationship terms and conditions I had ever heard of. They included only seeing friends once a week, no drinking after 10:00 pm, no talking to the moms of his son's youth hockey teammates, always sharing GPS location via text, and much, much more.

Despite all of that, Greg was very high-functioning. I actually think he would have scored well on an IQ test if given one. He had an extensive vocabulary and interesting takes on things. He was very quick-minded. But regardless of his potentially high IQ, it was evident he had never learned how to apply it in everyday life. He experienced frequent mood swings as well, quite possibly stemming from an undiagnosed case of bi-polarity. It happened to be flaring up on this particular Monday morning.

"Greg," I say as a greeting with a tight nod as I settled into my desk. Greg responded likewise but with an extra detail,

"Christopher, you're six minutes late."

"Oh, I'm sorry it affects you to the point of having to mention it."

"We are all held to the same standard. You're no better than me. You think I don't want six extra minutes to myself? Society has rules and so does this office. I could've stayed in my car to rub one out in six minutes if this office didn't have easy-to-follow set hours."

Greg often thought he was Larry David's offspring, or mentee perhaps. He enjoyed pointing out things other people found too uncomfortable or awkward or sensitive to mention. Things that didn't necessarily have anything to do with him, but with society in general. He was never uncomfortable speaking out, that's for sure. Greg and I were good friends, but he treated me no differently than a stranger in line with him at the DMV.

"Why are you being so cunty?" I asked. "Bad weekend?"

"My weekend was fine."

"'Fine' is a verbal cry for help—it stands for fucking incapable of normal emotions," I said, prompting Jill to put in her headphones.

"But I am fine. Just no excitement. Much like life in general. No stimulus. Maybe I'll join a pickleball league. I don't know. I need another meaningless fling with a hockey parent."

Greg said all this in a flat monotone, staring at his computer and never making eye contact with me. He also never lowered his voice when saying something oddly personal. He was self-aware, but just didn't seem to care. The fling with a hockey parent was in reference to a love affair with the mother of one of his son's hockey teammates. Most people my age did not call these instances 'love affairs' but the woman in question was significantly older—in her late 40s—so it seemed appropriate.

We made our way to the Monday morning meeting. They were held every week, a half-hour after the workday began. The purpose was to go over ongoing projects and new prospects as well as help with ad ideas and marketing concepts. Everyone went around the room to go over updates on accounts and anything pertinent to business in general. Once that was completed, we also went around the room and everyone had to volunteer their 'win' of the weekend. A personal victory we had experienced or something fun we did with friends or family outside of work. This was our owners' half-assed, occasionally excruciating attempt to give the office a fun environment and get to know everyone else on a more personal level. I usually made mine up. I had no interest in divulging to my co-workers that I ate sushi and had drunk sex with a borderline stranger in her overpriced, handicapped-bathroom-stall-sized Clayton apartment on Friday night. Despite my overall dislike for sharing my updates and my 'win', I still loved the weekly tradition because I got to hear Greg's commentary. Greg did not play well with a lot of people in the office, so he was always reluctant to speak in company meetings despite his Larry David-esque qualities. He did not want to waste time talking to these people. Nonetheless, he had to participate. Holistically and in theory, his job was important to him in terms of having a job. It was not necessarily important in that he worked hard and wanted to do his best.

Our VP of Sales Strategy motioned over to Greg, "All right Greg, what was your win?"

"I went and saw the movie *The Nun*. It was terrible."

"So how is that a win?"

"Because I got out of the house."

4

I have never been a very big proponent of the various dating apps out there. I preferred to meet women in person because messaging is a terrible medium for getting to know someone. I will admit to the brilliance of finding people to hook up with while sitting on the toilet, but photogenically speaking I often looked like a highly deranged pervert, so apps like Tinder did not benefit me in any discernible way. In almost every photo I looked dead behind the eyes. I portrayed someone who had dozens of kidnapped children locked up in cages in a windowless, soundproof basement, and a collection of women's heads in the freezer, à la Patrick Bateman.

When I met women it was usually in bars. Occasionally I would meet a cute girl, we would have a wonderful conversation, she would wholeheartedly give me her number, and I would text her... and I would do all this only to never hear back from that girl again. Which is enough to drive a guy into an insanitarium.

Why did women do this? Do girls have any idea how many men they have banished to a life of paralyzing self-doubt and insecurity? And before calling me sexist, I will admit guys do it to women as well, but it just seems cruel when guys do it. Even I, a victim of this mind-fucking tortuous pastime, will admit that it is kind of funny when women do it, while not ideal. I guess that is the definition of a double standard and therefore kind of sexist. Whatever.

So, to further divulge—I was downtown on a Friday night with a few friends at some pseudo-country dance bar that played shitty Luke Bryan songs and everyone cheered when drunk people were flung off a mechanical bull. We were posted up at the bar with backs facing the barkeeps. Oozing vibes. Sniffing out the estrogen-infused musk of all the women who walked by. I had my head on a swivel looking for potential lovers like an oscillating fan you set up in the hot summer months because you're too cheap to turn on the air con.

After a short while, a cute girl approached me. At the time, my dumb drunk brain thought that she stood in front of me solely so I would start talking to her. I thought she dug my enticing vibrancy. In retrospect, she was probably just trying to get a drink and I was in her way. But that is neither here nor there.

I opened with, "Hey, how's your life?" in honor of the illustrious George Costanza and we start talking. Her name was Jamie, which I loved because it allowed me to use the word 'androgynous,' which made me sound smart despite being kind of an idiot. We talked for what I believed to be 20–30 minutes. The intense chemistry and flirtatious banter gave me a mental boner. Romance was in the air. But this girl was one of the good ones, so when our conversation ended, she respectfully said she had to go home and simply gave me her number. No coitus with strangers. She oozed class. I think I loved her.

Cut to Sunday afternoon. After a few Shiner Bocks and a couple games of Blokus at a Soulard neighborhood bar to keep my mind sharp, I decided to send her a message. I always tried to reach out within 48-hours of meeting someone because I had been told that I was inordinately forgettable. In composing that text, I simply introduced myself as the halfwit she met on Friday night, made a couple light jokes, complimented her, and asked her out for a drink. I didn't want a text conversation, I wanted to see her again. Laid-back yet to the point. Very tasteful. It's not a science, it's an art form. I select send. You sly debonair text machine, I think to myself…

No response.

This was perplexing and a hearty strike to the face but I was not yet down for the count. Maybe she was busy. Also, girls play mind games. Not fun board games like Blokus. Some girls want a guy to border on embarrassing himself to get her attention before they respond. There are a lot of smart and pretty sociopaths out there. These kinds of girls like to prove their worth, then add tax, then shortchange you.

On the other hand, sometimes they're just not that interested. If that's the case, sending a second text is like a homeless guy asking somebody for a dollar, being told no, and then coming back and asking for $500. But I didn't care. So I waited another 24 hours to text her again. A second text is okay if done properly. Self-deprecation and humor work well in these instances and have proven successful in the past. If you can make a girl laugh you can make her do anything (butt stuff).

So I sent her a follow up text to my date request saying, *I'll take that as an emphatic maybe.*

Another day went by from this display of non-reciprocated affection and there was still no response. I gawked at the now seemingly pathetic text thread.

While I was very discouraged and confused, I would not give up. Why not you ask? Like, take the fucking hint Chris. Why not move on? Admit defeat. There are plenty of beavers in the river. Well, I'll tell you why I couldn't move on. Because I was now in love with this girl. If she texted back immediately and we went out, maybe she's nothing special, but in direct correlation to the George Costanza theory, which was a variation on the Groucho Marx edict of 'I do not care to belong to a club that accepts people like me as members', I was suddenly filled with passionate love for her. I could not resist the allure of a girl who was not interested in me. It was intoxicating. If you had me retake the Rorschach test at that moment, every inkblot would have just looked like Jamie's face. Or a penis. They mostly all look like penises.

So I thought to myself, what could I possibly do at this point to make her respond to me? It's clear I was far from anything even resembling an expert, but I knew that two texts are the absolute max you can send. Two can work, but three only makes matters worse. More texts would be like trying to put out a housefire with a teacup. I instead chose to change the approach. Texting girls and liking their Instagram photos is for teenage milksops, I decided. With less than a grain of actual logic, I determined that I needed to call her.

I told myself at that moment that in exactly two days I would dial her number, which would undeniably go straight to her voicemail. Sometimes a two- or three-line text can't revamp the great conversation and chemistry that was shared when first meeting. It's possible the girl may have forgotten the feeling of attraction she felt at the time or is too coy to text back. I was technically a stranger, so to her or anyone in general it's fair to ignore me.

It is also likely that some women may be too nervous or put-off by a phone conversation with a guy they barely know, but a woman that can't hold a conversation without gifs, acronyms, and emojis is not worth knowing anyways. I truly believed the tone of your voice and audible presentation can remind her why she inserted her full name and presumably genuine number into your phone in the first place. I had nothing to lose by calling; my dignity had been absent for years already. Choosing the inverse, I would never hear from this sandy-haired cutie again anyway. And if a phone call didn't work, I knew plenty of sites on the dark web that could do background checks for next to nothing to find her address. I would just show up at her apartment, possibly under her bed. Now that's romantic.

5

The following week at work went slowly. Eight women on Monday's walk. Only six on Tuesday. Sitting at my desk on Wednesday afternoon I casually mentioned aloud that I could use a drink. Greg immediately sprung at the chance to see more of me. "I would grab a couple happy hour drinks and some food after work, Christopher."

"Okay, but only if you stop calling me Christopher and I choose the venue."

"Okay."

Without deliberation I chose Tani Sushi. It was my favorite restaurant and I knew they didn't have much of a happy hour so Greg would have to pay full price for his drinks. I would too, but his perceptible indignation when receiving his bill would be a fair monetary payoff.

"Sushi?! I have never had sushi in my life. I do not want raw fish Christopher," Greg squawked in discontent when hearing the proposed location.

"It'll be fun. You said you needed excitement in life. Try some sushi."

We arrived and when ordering drinks, Greg asked the waitress to list all their available beers, both on tap and bottled. After she listed roughly 15 different options Greg said, "Okay, I'll just have a Bud Select." He did this every time I ever went somewhere with him. He always knew a Bud Select is exactly what he planned to order but needed to feel like he had different options—a psychological issue, I'm sure—so he made the wait staff painstakingly list every single choice on the menu, only to resort back to Bud Select without fail.

"Why do you always do that?" I asked.

"Good to know your options. Maybe I'll switch it up on number two." Of course he wouldn't and didn't. After reading almost every sushi roll description out loud with snide commentary to follow, Greg finally chose three dishes from the menu. They were the three inexpensive rolls. We chatted and drank while waiting for our food.

"So why don't you like talking during the Monday morning meeting?" I asked.

"I'm afraid of letting out a Freudian slip." Distracted easily, Greg started noticing other people's meals coming out from the kitchen. "I thought the whole thing was that it was supposed to be raw, why is everything coming out on fire?" I was not sure if he was talking to me or having a moment to himself. He continued, "I'm not using those stupid sticks. This is America. I'm using a fork. If I ever go to Japan, I will try to figure it out." Minutes went by and he announced this again, "I'm serious, I'm not going to use those damn sticks. I want a fork. Actually, just give me a pair of needle-nose pliers." About three drinks and 15 minutes later our food arrived. Greg was beginning to become inebriated and noticeably more upset about the utensils. "I need a fork!" he said to no one in particular. No one responded, so he repeated himself. "Hello? I need a fork. I don't know how to use these sticks." Still no one acknowledged his grievance. In an uncharacteristic fashion, Greg gave up, "Okay, I guess I'll try these fucking sticks." As almost everyone does their first time, Greg thoroughly enjoyed sushi. He confirmed this verbally to me. "Who knew uncooked fish could be so good. Might try raw chicken next." Midway through the meal we ordered sake and were taking shots until we paid the bill. He was too drunk to notice the lack of happy hour specials. While the night was ultimately uneventful, I think it did Greg some good. His life was so dull and repetitive that something as simple as going for sushi gave him a sense of vitality. He drank enough to deem himself inoperable behind the wheel so we Ubered back to the city. I told him I could drive him to his car in the morning. We got into the cab and the Uber driver asked, "So, were you guys out celebrating anything special tonight?" Greg quickly answered, "Yeah, we were out eating raw fish."

After first dropping Greg off at his parents' house, the Uber made its way downtown where I found myself with a nice buzz from the alcohol but no one to share it with. I decided to use it to my advantage. After a couple drinks, your brain shuts off in certain areas, but creativity heightens in others as the endorphins begin to plow. This is why some writers and musicians drink and micro (or macro) dose for inspiration. Another benefit in a flawlessly executed buzz is one's nervousness in social situations is often relinquished. As I leaned over my kitchen island table, I pulled out my phone and scrolled to Jamie's name. For roughly five minutes I mentally constructed an articulate, if not especially amusing, message to leave and prepared myself for the rarity of a conversation if she answered. I took a deep breath and courageously pressed call.

6

I called her. I will preface by saying I have gone up to hundreds of women I did not know at bars and never once felt nervous. I even went up to actress Kristy Swanson once at a casino in Las Vegas without a quiver. However, I only knew her as Christie Boner from the comedy *Dude, Where's My Car?* and had no idea she was well-known or in any other movies. Looking back, I don't think I was technically hitting on her, but here is how our interaction went:

Drunk 21-year-old Chris: Hey, are you Christie Boner?

Christie Boner: Yeah... wait, is that what you recognize me from?

Drunk 21-year-old Chris: Yeah, I've watched that movie about a hundred times. You were great. Should I know you from something else?

Christie Boner: *walks away*

Well excuse me! Get off your high horse, you hot piece of pompous ass. You're the one who took a role where the character's last name was *Boner*. Be proud of your work. I subsequently IMDb'd her and to be fair she was in quite a few notable movies beforehand such as *Big Daddy, Ferris Bueller's Day Off, Buffy the Vampire Slayer* among others, but *Dude, Where's My Car?* was a cinematic gem. What are you so pissy about? She was also in *Pretty in Pink*, but it was a non-speaking role. Yeah, like I'm going to recognize the blonde dink who didn't say anything. Whatever.

Nevertheless, calling the girl I met in the bar after two non-responsive texts, I was absolutely trembling despite the liquid courage. It predictably went to voicemail, but I was ready. The message was psychotically scripted beforehand. It was possibly funny, but I was unsure if it was funny enough to change someone's mind on ever wanting to see me again. It was also possible that it was *unfunny* enough for her to have a restraining order filed. The verbal memorandum was as follows:

Hey Jamie, this is Chris—the somewhat funny but not really kinda cute idiot you met on Friday night. Cute like... I don't know... a mangy three-legged dog or something. At any rate I was hoping to try out this new bar in Benton Park tomorrow, wanted to see if you'll join me... Would be cool to see you again but at this point I'll settle for a "Fuck off Chris, I'm not interested." That would actually be great. Let me know.

After I left the message, I thought to myself, if I don't hear back from her I will never know what happened between the short time period of getting her number and now. I think since this had happened a few times to me, it was possible I was blacking out for the last 10 seconds of the conversation and saying something so dog shit that it completely offset whatever great conversation we had prior to that point, eradicating the impression I made.

So right after I say 'Yeah, I'll call you', I maybe had been following it up with something like:

I think mass genocide was a great idea. We need a new age Hitler.

Or:

They were called Adam and Eve, not Adam and STEVE. Gay marriage makes me sick.

Or maybe:

Wanna get out of here? I am hung like a sardine.

Or even:

I think guac *should* be extra. I don't understand what everyone bitches about. It's an addition to the meal.

All those comments are equally offensive. Only one of those statements was true in my mind but I am not revealing which one.

The rest of Wednesday, Thursday, and Friday all went by without word from my dream inamorata. I felt like a well-behaved house pet who had been spontaneously struck by their drunk owner simply for showing love and affection. So confused. So hurt. So embarrassed. I'll never understand it, I thought.

Early that Friday evening I decided to take an impromptu road trip for the weekend to Nashville to ease my failed attempts at wooing, maybe meet some strange Midwestern ass. My friends Daryl and Jim came with me as we all had a mutual friend in Nashville with a free place to crash. My 22-year-old self would have probably hoped that by the age of 29 I was not sleeping on friends' stained and non-vacuumed floors anymore. Optimistically I would instead be at the point in my life where I stay in hotels or guest rooms of successful home-owning friends, but that was far from the case.

I was able to sneak out of work early like most Fridays and we left St. Louis around 4:00 pm. That morning I spotted 13 women on my walk that I wanted to plow. We got to our friend's place just 10 minutes outside of Broadway St. by about 9:00 pm. Our friend Miles just finished basic training in the Army an hour or so outside of Nashville and was now working in a bar called Tequila Cowboy during the weekdays. Miles was a tall, fit, well-groomed, bald black guy. Picture a dark-skinned Mr. Clean with a sailor's lexicon and a curious interest in bondage. His apartment was ill-decorated with eggshell white walls. There were no photos or pictures on display, just a poorly mounted 47-inch TV with a spaghetti of wires hanging out of the back of it. Miles had just enough seating for a few guests, which included a three-cushion, felt maroon couch, a dirty brown recliner, and a dining room table with four wooden chairs that looked like it was from the set of *That '70s Show*. Only two of the wooden chairs matched. Upon our arrival Miles had two girls over who were kind of unfortunate looking but seemed kind of fun. They had already been drinking for a couple of hours, as had we on the drive over. We pre-gamed for a solid hour while getting to know each other and determined our plans for the evening. The girls' names were Girl A and Girl B. Okay, I can't remember their names, so henceforth it's Girl A and Girl B. They started talking about the Lindsey Vonn nudes that were recently leaked from her hacked phone in August 2017.

"Oh my god and she had all these photos where she's completely naked except for her snowboarding boots. I was dying," said either Girl A or Girl B. I interjected myself into the conversation.

"Who gives a fuck about Lindsey Vonn nudes? You're totally burying the lead on that whole ordeal. Did you see the photo of Tiger Woods' meat pipe that was on her phone? If door number one is 100 photos of a naked Lindsey Vonn, and door number two is one photo of Tiger Woods standing awkwardly with his dick hanging out, I'm choosing door number two. Every. Single.

Time."

"I think you might be gay," Girl A retorted.

"Am I attracted to Tiger Woods? No. At least not sexually, but I must know what one of the greatest athletes of our generation's wrench looks like. And he did not disappoint. What a barber's pole."

The girls were now laughing and enjoying my presence, but they were still breathtakingly unattractive. I decided I needed to drink more. I asked Miles what he had for shots. Turns out it's a choice between Crown Royal Green Apple or some off-brand tequila. I was perplexed why any sensible Canadian whiskey company would create such an abortion of a flavor and quickly went for the tequila. We all did a round. The girls were starting to look more agreeable. So were the guys.

With a consensus that it was time to venture to Broadway Street, I stayed silent until someone else mentioned that we needed an Uber. Thanks for volunteering, I thought to myself. It was Girl A. She ordered the ride and I could tell she was proud of herself for contributing something to the group. I have always tried to avoid this type of gesture because no one ever remembers. Purchases might include rounds of shots, cab fares, and cover charges, among other miscellaneous drinking costs. Very few people ever remember these moments when you whip out your wallet in triumph and declare, "I got this." It seems like an honorable and admirable act at the time but within five minutes no one cares or even remembers. And I'm not doing anything nice for people if they don't care or remember. Buying a round of shots isn't a good enough deed to make me feel decent intrinsically. It's not exactly comparable to donating money to unfortunate kids in Sri Lanka. All these assholes have money and are just getting drunk. I think there's even a famous saying about it. Generosity killed the cat or something.

I liked to sit up front in the Uber because the drivers were usually interesting people for whatever reason. I would ask them a slew of generic questions to try to find out why their life has gone down the path of ferrying drunks around town for a living (which isn't so bad, by the way).

Our driver was a good-looking, younger guy in his early 30s, with short sunflower blond hair. He was a firefighter in his day job. When moderately buzzed, I could get to the core of a person in conversation. Suddenly, we were talking about his recent divorce. His name was Tim and he was hurting. I certainly could not relate but I knew when a person needed to get laid, guy or girl. I asked Tim if he wanted to come in the bar and drink with us. I was also very coercive when drinking and he eventually obliged. He parked the car a few blocks away and we all went into a bar called Whiskey Bent Saloon on Broadway. I strayed towards the back of the group just in case someone wanted to be a hero and buy all the covers. Turned out Whiskey Bent wasn't charging a cover that night.

The absence of an entry fee was very evident when we entered. There was a shortage of patrons to start with, and the first man that looked at me had the googliest eye I had ever seen. He looked like a cartoon crypt keeper. I gave him the quintessential white-person-half-smile-paired-with-a-head-nod and walked on. The bar line was scarce, if not non-existent, so I went on the far side to avoid paying for the others. I felt a halfway decent buzz at the apartment and in the car but immediately in this

Broadway environment I felt as sober as a teetotaler. I ordered a shot of rail bourbon and a Miller Lite for no ostensible reason other than it was the first beer I saw. There was a girl to my right at the corner of the bar. She appeared to have all her teeth, so I casually approached her as I waited for my degenerate drink order. "Hey, how's your life?" I asked.

She smiled, "You know, my life's kinda crazy lately to be honest! I just moved here a few months ago to be a musician and I turned 27 today!"

Why did people feel the need to tell everyone that it was their birthday when they're out? I'm sorry but you didn't accomplish anything amazing. Everyone in the entire fucking world has a birthday. You could not be less special for having one too. Your parents had sex and you've managed not to die. That is what a birthday symbolizes.

She did not ask me for my negative opinion on birthdays, so I decided to keep these thoughts to myself. I instead went a different route with the conversation that failed miserably.

"Oh, well hopefully you die this year then. If you're any good at music you will die at 27—all the best artists do. Jim Morrison, Amy Winehouse, Hendrix, Joplin, Cobain—all counting worms when they were 27 years old."

"Umm... are you telling a girl you just met that she should die this year? That is, like, super rude and creepy."

"Yeah, I suppose it is. Nice meeting you." I took my whiskey shot as she stared at me in condemnation and then I went back to the group.

"That girl was kinda cute, what happened there?"

asked Jim.

"I think I told her to kill herself."

"Smooth."

We finished our drinks and in complete unanimity decided this bar was not our scene. We walked down Broadway for about 30 seconds until we went around the corner to a bar called Nudie's Honky Tonk. I ignored two beggars on the way. It's my money, get a job. Nudie's was an elongated never-ending bar with various eclectic decor on the walls, like framed country singers' stage outfits and even a full-sized convertible car. It was a very appealing atmosphere and an abundance of customers at the time, including a bachelorette party. I turned to Tim the Uber driver, Daryl, Jim, and Miles, "You peckerheads ready to offend that entire group of girls with off-color comments?"

"Yup."

"Absolutely."

"Let's do it," they all said in unison. Except Tim. He was not sure how to answer so he remained silent.

Girl A and Girl B had their own agenda, which I believe was obtaining free drinks from strange men, so we grabbed a round of brews and shots and crashed their bachelorette party.

"Hey girls, who's the poor decision-maker that's getting married?" I asked. A few of the girls laughed and a couple looked at me with contempt. The rest of the brain-dead merrymakers seemed ambivalent to the opening line.

"This bitch right huurrrrrrr!" said a decent-looking Latino woman as she pointed at the bride-to-be.

"We are actually on a scavenger hunt. We could probably use you guys to knock something off this list," the poor decision-maker said.

"All right, let me see it," I said. I started to scan the list and they were about halfway through with the majority of the easy or fun items crossed off. I started to read them aloud. "Number 24: find a virgin. Daryl, these girls need you for the scavenger hunt." Daryl responded by mumbling something about orgasms. I continued reading items off the list. "Number 40: find the cheesiest guy in the place and ask him if he's getting lucky. Daryl, these girls really need you for the scavenger hunt." Daryl again was not amused. The girls officially found me funny. "Number 52: ask a cute guy for hemorrhoid cream. Daryl isn't cute but he definitely has hemorrhoids."

"Those cleared up months ago," Daryl said as he belatedly began playing along in the hopes of sex with drunk bachelorettes. After a couple more jokes in line with Daryl being gay or a virgin, but definitely not both, I opted for number 31: get a guy to do a shot of tequila off your chest. Somehow this one was still available. I ordered two shots of tequila. One for her because I am a nice person and placed the other one in the center of her bottomless cleavage. She clinked shot glasses and I encompassed the entirety of the rim of the glass in my mouth, buried my face playfully between her breasts as a little treat for myself, and then tilted my head back and took the shot. That was pretty much the height of interaction with this group as they wandered off shortly after to fulfill other meaningless scavenger hunt challenges.

Girl A and Girl B came back over with full drinks and started flirting with Tim the Uber-driving firefighter. As the rest of us were watching this, Miles leaned in and whispered, "The girls told me they are impressed by Tim's job and it's a turn-on."

"I agree," I replied, "driving for Uber is very heroic and selfless."

We left those three to chat about Tim's courageous career choice and went to check out the live band. There was a decent amount of people in front of the small stage, but it was not overcrowded. The band had just finished playing a David Allan Coe cover when I noticed a very intoxicated older gentleman screaming something to the lead singer about Wagon Wheel.

"Hey man! PLAY FUCKIN' WAGON WHEEL!" The band ignored his request and started playing a Charlie Daniels Band cover. They finished that song and the drunk guy was still yelling about playing Wagon Wheel. I was pretty sure that he never actually stopped yelling about it, but he could only be heard when the band wasn't playing. "Hey! Do you guys know Wagon Wheel or what? We wanna hear sum fuckin' Wagon Wheel!"

After about the fifth demand from drunk guy, they finally responded. Away from the mic I could hear the lead singer say, "Yeah dude, we can play Wagon Wheel." For those that don't know, Wagon Wheel is one of the easiest songs ever to play live. It is the same four chords the entire song. Truthfully, it's a fantastic number but drunk guy repeatedly asking to hear it was comical.

The band played the song and the drunk guy danced throughout, singing the lyrics poorly. Five minutes after they were done playing it, he started yelling at them again. "Hey shitheads, when the fuck are yew gonna play Wagon Wheel?!"

"We just played it, dumbass. Somebody get this guy

out of here." Drunk guy was promptly escorted out of the bar.

Shortly after, I grabbed the girls and had them join Miles, Daryl, Jim, and me. We finished our drinks and decided to go to our final destination bar: Rippy's further up Broadway. As we started walking in, I noticed a cute girl look at me and she held eye contact. This was more than enough to get me to approach the fairer sex, almost automatically and without conscious thought. Holding eye contact from a distance meant interest. Often there is eye contact without holding—I learned this is not necessarily an indicator of interest. I discovered this in high school after unceremoniously asking out a substitute teacher after class.

Back to cute Rippy's lady. Usually when I approached a woman at a bar, I used an opener a little obscure to engage in conversation. It never had the appearance of a pick-up line, just initiated a conversation. Yet approaching with locked eye contact is a much different scenario than the blind approach. In a blind approach, I needed to give her a reason to engage by being different and interesting. In these rare occurrences of eye contact, she is for some reason attracted to me physically. I began with the cutest "Hi" she'd ever heard. "Hi!"

"Hi," she responded. She was already personality mirroring me. Another sign of interest. I continued, "I'm not a cool guy or anything but I'd love to waste your time if you're interested." I stole this line from Larry David on *Curb Your Enthusiasm*. For some reason a lot of younger women didn't watch that show or *Seinfeld*, so I was never in danger of them calling me out.

"Do you waste a lot of girls' time?"

"If you were to ask them, yes. If you ask me…

probably, yeah."

"So you're a player?" She literally said 'player' like it was 1995.

"No, not at all. Just romantically retarded."

She laughed and became a bit more comfortable. Her name was Tara and she was an account manager for some boring company that offered a boring service for other boring companies. She asked what I did for work. I hated the question. I always made something up on the spot. "I own a gay bar in St. Louis called Bottoms Up." She didn't understand the double entendre joke and took me seriously, so I started talking about the hardship of owning a bar and the struggle of continuing to earn a steady margin of profit. I had watched so much *Bar Rescue* that I could talk as fluently as a real owner. I taught her about the industry, pointing out things Rippy's did well and things they did poorly. After about 15 minutes I solidified her as an option for the night and even as a chance to see Saturday, so I promptly asked for her number and excused myself back to the group.

Girls B and A were off talking to a batch of guys in cowboy hats and plain white T-shirts tucked into their bootcut Levis. Miles, Daryl, and Jim were talking to a group of six girls from Indianapolis. Two of them were having their own conversation together while the other four were hanging off every word and crappy joke my idiot friends were saying.

Introductions were made and the drunken conversation continued. Of the four girls, three were cute, physically fit, and blonde in their early 20s. The fourth was around 5'10", had an unbecoming face, picket-fenced teeth, and the body of Newt Gingrich. *I bet she's a great Division III college volleyball player*, I thought to myself. I started taking notice to what was happening in front of me. The three attractive girls were latched onto Jim, Daryl, and Miles. The fourth, Lisa, knew this too and showed no timidity towards her interest in me. She had a desperate, last-ditch-effort-at-the-bar type of fascination in me. This happened from time to time. All three of my friends were in the military and considered hot guys. Daryl and Jim looked like bull-necked bodybuilders. Miles was the most handsome black man in Tennessee, ranking well ahead of the other eight. I came to the party late, so being stuck with butter face was something I'd have to deal with.

"Hey, I'm Lisa."

"Hey, I'm Eugene, pleasure is all yours," I said dispassionately.

"They said your name is Chris..."

"What the fuck do they know?"

She laughed and continued calling me Chris. Everything I did to try to repulse this girl while simultaneously trying to amuse myself seemed useless. The more of an asshole I was, the more interested she became. It was infuriating but also quite interesting in terms of social experiments.

"So what do you do, Chris?"

"I write, like... children's books... but they're for senile elderly people."

"Ha ha, sounds like a fun job. So you're single?"

"I guess."

"I find that hard to believe," she said. I felt a compliment coming on, so I took the bait.

"Why do you say that?"

"You're funny and you're cute. Can't imagine girls aren't all over you every weekend."

"Women find me exhausting," I said in a monotone voice, not looking at her. "I also have a tiny dick."

"Ha ha, I'm sure you do! What do you do for fun?"

"Sometimes I wander the streets for days to try to understand the mindset of homeless people. I also drink and do drugs, mainly hallucinogens."

"You are funny. Not that great at flirting though," she said with a gross smile. I also think she attempted to wink but her eyelid just fluttered like it was having a spasm.

"I'm actually pretty good at flirting, you just haven't seen me in action. If I was a lesbian, I'd be all over you."

As the conversation and drinks continued it become very evident that we were leaving with these girls. They too were in Nashville for a spontaneous weekend break and were staying at an Airbnb nearby. They were all allegedly single aside from the two probable lesbians who hadn't spoken to us at all. We ordered a couple Ubers and went back to their rented apartment. We convened in the kitchen before slowly two-by-two couples started disappearing off into the bedrooms. I looked up from my 5% battery signal on my phone to see my two o'clock beauty queen staring at me lasciviously. There was another problem on top of this. All the bedrooms were taken. I had to share the couch with this homely young woman.

As we settled on the couch, I looked at her. I was drunk yet coherent. She appeared awkward and oafish. I did not care. In fact I rarely cared. We started making out. This had become mechanical over the years. Little concentration was needed, so my mind started racing when I was kissing a girl. I started to think about the most irrelevant things. Squirrels, Chinese people, the layout of the room I was in and how it could be better if they moved the couch against the adjacent wall, Mindy Kaling's swelling success, why glue doesn't stick to the inside of a bottle, the buoyancy of oil, squirrels again, and eventually how I wanted the rest of this scenario to play out. In my mind I was thinking how I did not desire to have sex with her, but I wanted her to do things with my penis. We started removing clothes. A shiesty move I would often do was lean away from the girl, put my head back and arch my spine as if I was stretching. This was a non-verbal cue for oral sex, yet it's not outright. I was not directly asking for a blowjob, not even implying it, but something about that motion and body configuration speaks to the potential giver. It was as if, hey, look what we have here, it's so close—why not try it? This half-baked maneuver somehow worked and Lisa ended up giving me a weak-kneed blowjob, although it was definitely not lacking enthusiasm. I came in her mouth and went into the bathroom to do nothing really, I just wanted to let her know the sexual encounter was over. Any woman who has ever had a random hook-up with a guy knows that when he comes that carnal session is over. Guys are unilaterally selfish. Any man who comes and then proceeds to reciprocate oral sex to a stranger is a disgusting pig. Or possibly a very altruistic and giving person. Whatever. Traditionally, if you want head ladies, make sure it's before your partner climaxes.

I went back into the living room, grabbed a three-foot wool afghan from a recliner, and laid down on the floor. "You're not going to sleep on the couch with me?" she asked with a hint of sadness.

"I am not. Back problems. Will you toss me a pillow?"

I was always a habitual early waker after drinking. Turns out the alcohol from the previous night, or just hours before in several cases, ignites something in the brain to become wide awake first thing. It disrupts your REM cycle. So even after going to bed sometime around 3:00 am, it was now 6:45 and I was wide awake. Everyone else in the house was naturally still asleep. To avoid laying on the floor for two hours alone with my freakish thoughts, I got up, chugged some water, scavenged the medicine cabinet for ibuprofen, and sat in the kitchen for a few minutes. My phone was dead. I walked into the living room and noticed a few books on the shelf. I grabbed *Girl on the Train* by Paula Hawkins and sat in a chair on the front patio. I got 40 pages in before the other guys awoke and start sneaking out. The book was good, so I stole it. We said our awkward goodbyes knowing we would never see these women again and scurried out. There were a couple comments from the girls about grabbing breakfast, but we pretended not to hear them. Lisa sat idly by waiting for me to get her number but I left without a backward glance. What a jerk. As we stood outside waiting for the Uber, we looked back to ensure the blinds were closed and then proceeded to high-five each other like the douchebags that we were.

What happened that night was rare in a bachelor group's existence. Going out as a crowd of four and all getting laid in some way or another with a commensurate group of four female counterparts, that is. It is much more frequent in a pair of a friends, maybe even three. But four is unheard of; the ultimate loser-bro bonding experience.

Our Uber driver arrived and the sight of him made me think out loud, "Hey, what happened to Tim?"

7

The most underrated part of a weekend away with your friends can often be the mornings—the moments when you lounge around and reminisce about the events and absurd things said and done the night before. That was notably true this Saturday morning in Nashville. I was clearly the brunt of a few jokes regarding the bloated small power forward I fornicated with on the couch the night before, but I didn't care. Barring a sexual transmitted disease, it was usually worth the story and the weird experience. I loved meeting and interacting with new people, occasionally in a sexual way. Lisa was undesirable, but I still found something beautiful about her. I could usually uncover something unique and special in every woman I met. Whether it be their eyes, their intelligence, their outlook on life, or perhaps they had a spectacular ass and/or shapely melons. Lisa was no different. She had a certain inner beauty to her. A free spirit. Affability. Something, I don't know, we barely talked actually. I may have never wanted to see her again as long as I lived, or in whatever afterworld possibly but probably doesn't exist, but I didn't regret the hour on the couch with her and the mediocre blowjob. Now that is chivalry!

We were not sure what happened to the two girls we went out with the night before. Miles didn't seem concerned. I don't think he knew them well based on his apathy when I asked where they went. Hopefully they had a threesome with Tim the firefighting Uber driver, or Uber-driving firefighter. Whatever was politically correct.

The group was hungry and it was a gorgeous day. We decided the best plan of action was to grab brunch with some drinks and find a rooftop shortly after to commence daytime drinking—the best activity ever conceptualized for people without real friends or hobbies or families.

Brunch was fine. Uneventful. More reminiscing about the night before, which provoked a few laughs. We begrudgingly paid our stiff tourist city tabs and relocated to The George Jones. This was a bar with live music and a museum of the late singer. More importantly, it contained an elongated rooftop bar with views of the Cumberland River and the Titans' Nissan Stadium. The sun was beaming through the faint clouds and the view was glorious.

Just before 1:00 pm, the rooftop was already semi-filled. We found a spot at the brick-based and concrete-countered bar just next to a pair of oak whiskey barrels. We were all insightful, intellectual individuals, so naturally our highbrow group conversation caught the attention of the men and women near us.

"No way, dude! You can fuck one cartoon character and you're choosing a rabbit? That is bestiality, you sick fuck!" Jim said to Daryl's ridiculous answer to my 'Which cartoon character would you have sex with?' debate.

"Whatever. Lola Bunny is so damn hot, man." Daryl continued, "So it's okay to have sex with a fictitious character people create on a piece of paper with colored pencils but it can't be an animal? What kind of bullshit logic is that? Who would you do?" He directed this to Jim, but I interjected. I had thought about this question before and had articulated an answer with substantial reasoning.

"Lois Griffin from *Family Guy*," I said straight-faced and without hesitation. "Normally when I see guys I don't know out-kicking their coverage with a superior looking girlfriend I am infuriated, but for Peter Griffin I just feel joy. Lois has the most aesthetically erotic curves I have ever seen on a female cartoon. Also! They hint in several episodes that Lois has bisexual experiences. *Hot.* She's also had her fair share of extramarital affairs, including one with my favorite president of all time, Bill Clinton, as well as a sexual encounter with her daughter Meg's boyfriend in one episode. She even took part in a pornographic film in college titled *Quest for Fur*, like I needed another reason." I was out of breath. People nearby were laughing and looking to join our conversation.

"How the hell do you know all of that?" asked Jim.

"Wikipedia," I said. "Also, I want to state that *The Little Mermaid* is a close second. Ever since *The Shape of Water* won Best Picture I kind of want to have sex with a fish. NOT AN ANIMAL!" I motioned to Daryl before he could call me out. "I'm not even sure what the correct term would be for that... pescasexual? Anatomically speaking, I'm not sure where I would put it, but at least I wouldn't have to worry about getting her pregnant. The only reason I'd choose Lois over her is because I heard Ariel has crabs... get it?" Miles chimed in with Velma from *Scooby Doo*, "The sexiest thing about a woman... is her mind," he purred.

"Isn't she a lesbian?" Jim said.

"Whatever. Makes me like her even more. The heart wants what it can't have. That perfect fitting boob-hugging sweater... that short skirt... high socks. Zoikes. I'd also let the Brown M&M's piece of chocolate ass melt in my mouth any day of the week..."

"What the fuck is wrong with you guys?" a girl nearby said, slightly laughing with her two friends. The three girls differed severely in looks and stature. In my social travels I often found groups of girlfriends to be vastly similar in their appearance and personality. It was like they met by mistaking the other person as a mirror. This is especially true with pairs of best friends. More times than not they look like long lost sisters that found each other at college. This group was different though, like they spun a random female generator machine three times with three very different outcomes and decided to be friends. The girl that first spoke was tall with large breasts and wavy chestnut hair. She seemed to be the most gregarious and outwardly fun. I later found out her name was Karen. Her first friend, Lindsay, was very petite in size with dark hair. She had a bit of an attitude that was somewhat becoming. She was quick in her smartass remarks and had a witch's grin when she belittled us. I was enamored. The cynical ones always intrigued me. The second friend, Ashley, was a little more heavyset but had a pretty face and intensely curly black hair. She had one of the best laughs I'd ever heard. It was like the cackle of an angel.

"That's a loaded question," I answered. "How about you girls? I know you've thought about this before. Don't be shy, it's completely normal."

"No, I have never thought about having sex with a cartoon character before, it's completely abnormal," Lindsay said with her beautiful mouth.

"Li Shang from *Mulan*," Karen said almost at the same time as Lindsay. "Without a doubt. He is fucking gorgeous." Ashley didn't give an answer until we badgered her, which finally prompted her to say, "Okay, I think Johnny Bravo is hot."

I liked these girls. I decided to test their tolerance for weird idiots at the bar and crank up the vulgarity.

"Yes! I love it, Ashley. He *is* hot. How about Wreck-It Ralph? You don't get the name Wreck-It Ralph from making passionate, gentle, tender love with one woman your whole life. He fucking WRECKS the ovum. And those hands... can you imagine getting fisted by that mongoloid?" I said this facing Daryl, Jim, and Miles so as to not project my fisting comment directly towards the girls. Such a considerate gentleman.

"Can you please never say ovum again?" quipped Lindsay.

"Fair request," I answered. "Or maybe Inspector Gadget? He could probably get you off from 50 yards away with that go-go arm." Ashley's gorgeous cackle hit a new pitch.

"I actually always thought Patti Mayonnaise's dad was kind of a DILF," Karen joked.

"Isn't he in a wheelchair?" asked Daryl in poor taste. We all looked at him in contempt.

"What, he can't be an attractive guy because his legs don't work? Go use the bathroom or something Daryl. Just try not to take the handicap stall. We know how you like to disrespect those lesser abled," I said in a dry delivery. "What about Stu Pickles?" I continued. "I bet that purple-haired freak fucks like a wild animal." I saw Lindsay give an audible laugh for the first time in the interaction.

"You are seriously fucked up," she said with a smile. Jim chimed in with another bad pun,

"How about Bullwinkle? I heard he's hung like a moose."

"I'd like to get gang-banged by the Ninja Turtles," Karen said.

We ended up moving into a nearby lounge area with the girls and ordered more drinks. They were genuinely funny. They all kind of had a Chelsea Peretti vibe to them that was attractive. We spent another hour drinking and conversing when I felt my phone vibrating in my pocket. In that current day and age, phone calls had a sense of urgency to them. People texted; they didn't call any more. It was a dying form of communication from a social point of view. The mystery of a phone call before checking the caller ID was always fascinating. I took my phone out of my pocket to take a brief glance, until it transformed into a prolonged gaze of euphoria… it was Jamie.

8

Jamie, you saucy minx. It was 3:18 pm on Saturday when the girl I had been fretting over for more than a week had presumably pocket-dialed me by mistake. Or became desperate. Or just got out of an eight-day coma. Or had her pretend boyfriend call me from her phone to tell me to kindly fuck off... who knew? I was in the loud rooftop bar so I couldn't pick up, but I couldn't stop smiling in disbelief staring at it as it rang. I suddenly realized I had never liked a girl this much in my entire life. I dated a chick intensely for two years in college and I never liked her as much as this girl I met half-drunk at a bar for 10 minutes. Acknowledging that I couldn't, or more correctly shouldn't, answer I decided I would call her back when we left. Or *maybe* I would casually play it slow and call her back a couple days later. Although there was nothing casual about creating a calendar event to call a woman. It would be virtually the opposite. Like a stalker who just happened to be in his victim's neighborhood. *Oh, you live here? Weird, I always walk by here at 2:00 am with binoculars and cable ties. How serendipitous is that?* It was too meticulous. Uncool. So I decided to call her back after The George Jones. My friends knew about Jamie and my pathetic attempt to woo her as I told them about it for amusement purposes. It seemed like a funny story at the time. But I was honestly stunned that the voicemail had worked. Although she left no return message, at that moment on the rooftop I was proud—feeling like an actual achievement—like I had won a free pint on the skee ball machine. The guys were in group conversation with our new female barflies, so I decided to hold off the news about the unforeseen call. Daryl was telling a story about how he got a blowjob in a mother's room during work hours at his old office internship. Clearly not a time to interrupt.

After another two hours of drinking and mingling, Karen, Lindsay, and Ashley left. They were locals and going to grab dinner. Without us. No phone number. No kiss goodbye. No "meet us later." Just a mere "good luck on the rest of your night and enjoy our city." We were used for our generosity and our hilarious jokes. Whatever. I lost interest in those foul-faced hookers the second I saw Jamie's name on my phone. As we walked outside I decided to call her back. I did not explain the situation to the guys, just floated away from them to make the call. Even after several drinks I was trembling. Again. But I knew what to say. I had a few jokes loaded in the chamber ready to pull the trigger on, but I never got the chance. A full six rings before reaching her voicemail. I missed my window. We got a ride back to Miles' to shower and change for the night. She did not call back. What kind of game was this? As for my next move... I had no idea. I had never tangoed like this before. All I knew was that I am outmatched. Whatever method Jamie was employing was next-level flirting and totally working. I was having a great time in Nashville, ready to move on, and then she did this.

I was so intrigued by this girl. I almost didn't want to meet her because I didn't want the titillation to end. But I knew I had to play it out because it had all the makings of America's next enchanting rom-com script. So the dance continued.

9

After a quick bite to eat from a nearby sandwich place and a brisk, manly primp, we were ready for Nashville round two. We had no female accompaniments so our pregame was a bit shorter. That and we had already been drinking frivolously for many, many hours.

The time spent at the bars was a bit of a haze, but the following were exchanges I had with women throughout the night:

Jim was talking to a girl. I turned to Daryl and said, "I weep for that girl. Watch this," I walked up to Jim and his victim and interrupted, "You know Jim, I never realized how small your hands are."

After speaking with a girl I was less than enthusiastic about, she said, "You should take down my number."

"Oh, I would but my battery is pretty low."

"What are you at?"

"71%."

I texted Tara, the girl from the night before who gave me her number. I received a text back that said, *Wrong number buddy.*

Talking to another girl at one point I interrupted her by saying, "All right enough about you, let's talk about me. I am really interesting." That was the end of the conversation.

One girl I coaxed out of the bar to go to a gift shop across the street with me. "I want to get something indigenous to the city," I announced. I ended up buying a black T-shirt that said 'Girls Nashville Weekend. Cheaper Than Therapy' in cursive pink font. I don't remember what happened to her.

You would think the more I talked to women and interacted with them, the better at it I would become. But every day my confusion grew. I proceeded to drink throughout the night, becoming overly intoxicated, mumbling dumb things to people while wearing some ridiculous XL female tourist shirt.

Later in the night I was kicked out of a bar by a very able-bodied bouncer. The band playing inside was looking for song requests to which I contributed. I asked the lead singer to play Werewolves of London by Warren Zevon. He said, "You got it, bud," and proceeded to play the song's riff, but then started singing the lyrics to All Summer Long by Kid Rock instead. I began taking cups and bottles out of the trash and throwing them on stage. I protested my innocence as the large bar worker tossed me out the front door while I kept yelling something about musical integrity.

Shortly after, Miles brought us to a weird house a 20-minute cab ride away. It was not a house I desired to live in or even visit for that matter. As we walked in there was a gentleman having sex with a young girl on the living room couch. Miles dismissed the scene nonchalantly. "Oh, don't worry about him, that's just Critter."

"I am worried about Critter," I retorted. Critter looked like a bald ex-prisoner who went to jail for blowing up his meth lab, and then later escaped. I explained my theory to Miles and he did not deny it.

"Oh yeah, he's a psycho, but a great guy to know."

I traditionally enjoyed living in the moment of spontaneity and finding amusement in every situation, but this was not one of those times. I wanted my bed. And while the house was weird, it was not as weird as the people in it. I decided to get an Uber and go back to Miles'. The poor girl who had just fucked Critter overheard me saying this and was also feeling uncomfortable. She asked to leave with me. I told her to ask Critter if it was okay. Not because men own the women they have semi-public sex with, but because I was afraid of him. She said he was dangerous when drunk and she was also afraid of him. I asked why she had sex with him. She said it was complicated. Sounded like forcible penetration by threat, but I suppose that would technically be considered complicated. I told her she could leave with me, but she had to wait five minutes after I left and sneak out without being seen. I didn't want Critter upset with me. My Uber arrived and I subtly exited through the front door with no one seeming to notice. I got in the car and told the driver we needed to wait five minutes for a girl to come out. She didn't wait five minutes. I think she waited seven seconds. Out came this girl running at full speed with Critter chasing her. She swiftly got in the car screaming and vehemently yelled at Manny, Red Honda Accord, 4.74 stars, to drive the fucking vehicle. Critter was half-naked running after our car and poor Manny had no idea what the hell was going on. Critter had an object in his hand. It appeared to be a knife. Stupid Critter.

We arrived at Miles' and I told her she could have the couch. The only thing I knew about her was that she liked the couch. I told her I was going to sleep on the floor. For a second night in a row, albeit unbeknownst to her. As I got situated, I suddenly heard rustling and turned over to see her trying to get under the covers with me. I pardoned her action. She then began grabbing my cock and telling me how thankful she was for saving her. About an hour ago I was so drunk I probably would've fucked a bag of potting soil. But meeting Critter and his house full of misfits was a very sobering experience. I was profoundly uninterested in getting whichever five or six sexual diseases Critter has inflamed her privates with. Her breath also smelled like the stale piss of 200 mules, probably from having Critter's prison dick in her mouth at one point. I stood up, excused myself, grabbed my stolen Paula Hawkins book, turned on the balcony light, and fell asleep in a chair on the deck reading. I was awoken an hour later by Miles, Daryl, and Jim returning from Critter's drug den. While I was half asleep Miles angrily explained that he could no longer talk to Critter ever again. "You're welcome," I said and went back to sleep on the porch.

A week later we all got a group text from Miles informing us that he saw Critter at the bar and that he couldn't remember anything from the Saturday night in question. They were still friends. Over the years I often wondered what Critter would eventually die from.

10

I had little concentration the following week at work. Jamie had clogged up my thoughts. This semi-anonymous mystery girl was either going to have to go on a date with me, willingly or not, or have her step-brother threaten me with critical violence. A lot had transpired in the few days prior. Twists in the plot had flexed and coiled. Frustration. Flirtation. Confusion. Joy. Arousal. Embarrassment. Impure masturbatory daydreams. All on my end. Not sure how she felt about any of this. Probably just annoyance. Luckily her thoughts and feelings didn't matter much.

When I got home from work that Tuesday, I decided to confuse myself even more and perform one last act of tender mortification. I thought about really upping the ridiculousness for my next move, such as sending an a cappella singing telegram to her office to perform 'Hungry Eyes' by Eric Carmen from the *Dirty Dancing* soundtrack. Or sending her a video resumé of myself on why I was such a viable dating candidate. But I realized I was too old-school and too humble for those harebrained yet possibly successful and funny ideas that could totally work. I decided to go with another call and likely another voicemail. It was my last-ditch effort. The

11th hour. My Hail Mary.

Normally I would not ask a girl out multiple times, but this one had my molecules jumping. I was officially desperate. The key when asking out a girl who's probably not interested in you is to suggest a specific outing each time. That way, if she doesn't respond or says no, or even, "Absolutely not, please leave me alone," she's technically only saying no to that specific date, not all dates. If you ask her, "Hey, want to go out sometime?" and hear nothing, you're finished.

So I called her again, like the quasi-Patrick Bateman that I am. Voicemail. The message was as follows:

What's up... I think you presumably pocket-dialed me by mistake last week. I was traveling so I couldn't answer and now I may never know why you called. But maybe... MAYBE you didn't pocket-dial me and you impulsively came to your senses and were considering seeing me again. At the very small probability of that, I'm calling to see if you want to grab dinner or drinks tomorrow night. Or live music. Anything. I will walk you to your fucking mailbox for a date. Give me something. If not, well, sorry I annoyed you with my friendship. All right, later.

So I waited. As impatiently as humanly possible. Waiting for responses was the worst part of the early stages of dating. Not the waiting specifically, but the not knowing. But at this point I was a little relieved for it to all be over. I did not want to admit defeat but there were legal issues at play if I continued. Harassment was a pressing issue in America, and I was becoming the poster boy for it.

Then it happened... a text message from Jamie.

Hey Chris, I appreciate your persistence! It's super flattering. I'm just going to be honest and tell you the reason I haven't replied is because I kind of remember meeting you at the bar but I'd be lying if I said I really remembered all that much. It's pretty embarrassing, but I was out celebrating that night and I just drank way too much!

We began a conversation. A couple witty jokes over here. Some flirtatious banter over there. "Ha ha oh you say that to all the girls I bet!" A good bit of back and forth. So I asked her if she wanted to get a drink with a stranger she scarcely remembered the following night. She said she would, if only I gave her my last name.

Good news and bad news. The obvious good news was that she agreed to go out with me, however with one caveat: send me your last name. I hated giving out my real last name. What did she want next? My social security number? I used a pseudonym on social media and booking hotels for a reason. I liked privacy. A concealed past. A separate identity. I even used a fictitious name when I wrote a blog in college. I posted under 'Dick Gozinya'. But for a date with this girl? I would obviously oblige. I figured she would Google me, but it ultimately wasn't a big deal. I sent her my last name: Van Zandt.

About 12 hours went by… crickets… tumble weeds…

At first, I didn't think much of it, but I started to wonder after half a day went by. I Googled 'Chris Van Zandt'.

Jesus Christ.

There were a few things I had to absorb. First off, she was clearly not impressed with small Division III college football records. She was also probably not impressed with past criminal charges—shallow much? Third and most importantly, when you Googled my real name only two very unflattering photos of me appeared. One being my freshman football headshot from 10 years ago. The other being my employee photo taken on my first day four years ago. I hated the internet.

In the first photo, I looked like someone who grew up

near a chemical power plant and chewed on wall insulation for breakfast. The second photo shown looked like the mug shot of a sedated troglodyte born out of incest who just escaped from a mental hospital. These descriptions were putting it nicely.

So when I realized this, I quickly sent her my Instagram name to give her a better idea of my looks, but it was too late. Or maybe it just added gasoline to the fire. My Instagram was basically just an accumulation of immature behavior, sex euphemisms, and off-key acoustic guitar covers badly captured on camera. I severely doubted it helped.

Days went by and I did not hear back. I knew I was not 'ugly' despite what all my closest friends and relatives said, but the rejection still hurt. It has been said that the better you look, the more you see... or something like that. I don't know. I decided to take a break from women. At least for the next 96 hours or so. I couldn't handle anymore. This girl was a queen and I loved her... but I wanted her to rot in hell. Turned out she was very shallow. But you know what? So was I. I would have done the same thing. God, we belonged together.

11

Attending a wedding unaccompanied has always had an unfair stigma attached to it—a severely misperceived byproduct of being single. I viewed the circumstance as a form of opportunism. I rarely brought dates because girls didn't text me back after Googling me for reasons already discussed, but also because being single and roaming around aimlessly at a place where you can smell the desperation for love is fun. And resourceful. The still single and despairing guests at a wedding see this beautiful love unified in front of them and instantaneously want it for themselves, making it a great place to meet someone as desperate and horny as you. To quote the great Russ Hanneman, "Don't bring sand to the beach, there's already pussy there."

However, when attending a wedding stag it's very likely that you know some of the other people who are also attending. In most cases you're there with friends and find yourself catching up with those you haven't seen in a while, almost to the point of annoyance at how many people you have to talk to. Well, on this particular Saturday night I was headed to a wedding downtown where I literally knew only the bride and groom. With that being said, this was one wedding where I would have loved to have brought a fun date... or even a local homeless woman. That way, I'd at least have someone to talk to, and no need to give her a ride to her place after. Yet there was no plus-one offered and that set the scene for the most awkward and lonesome cocktail hour of my life to date.

Traditionally I was pretty good at meeting new people and bonded quickly, but this was not a practical social setting. Showing up alone, not having one single person to mingle with while everyone else was there as a couple, is as awkward as it gets. It was not like starting a new job or being a freshman in college where relationships are opportune and nearly inevitable. This was like trying to make friends with strangers in the middle of a movie theater while the film is playing... or like breaking and entering someone's living room window while they are staring at you and you try to introduce yourself calmly. No one wants to meet some single loser by himself at a wedding. In order to cope with this ordeal, I decided to live tweet my night accordingly.

6:12: Going to a wedding & the only people I know are the bride & groom. Not sure how to interact. Will just drink until something suggests itself

6:20: Update: I'm just standing by myself near the bar, sipping a Jack & water... The barkeep is my only friend at the moment

6:24: I may try to make friends with the teenagers by getting them alcohol. They seem cool

6:25: There's a group of fun-looking youthful adults with an opening in their circle. I think I'll go up and make a joke about Colin Kaepernick to fit in

6:28: The faster I drink the quicker I can get back into the line at the bar. The drink line is a safe zone where I don't look alone

6:29: There's two barkeeps so if I alternate they won't get suspicious

6:31: Things are looking up. I just spoke to someone. Asked if she was in line. She said yes. More to come

6:46: People are starting to notice I have no friends. Getting sneers and hearing snickers. Dinner in 14 minutes

6:53: Photographer took last toasted ravioli. I told him the food is for the guests. He ignored me. This wedding is horse shit

7:09: Everyone at table nine is now my friend. My jokes are landing left and right

7:23: Said something offensive and lost all my friends at table nine

As the seated dinner portion concluded and the night wore on, I ended up getting half-in-the-bag drunk and having a decent time, but still left early and alone. The cocktail hour before dinner would forever be an all-time low point in my life.

Also, congratulations to Taylor and Claire. I hope they enjoyed the Bluetooth shower radio and stainless steel toilet brush I got them on the registry.

12

To alleviate my Sunday hangover, I decided to grab a bloody Mary in the early afternoon. Just one to ease my pain and make me feel normal. I descended to the breakfast bar called Blondie's below my apartment. By the second or third sip of my drink I decided I was going to imbibe all day. This was a purely carnal and unconscious decision that worried me a bit. I knew a few friends that participated in Sunday Funday just about every week. I texted one of them and within 12 seconds received a text that simply said, *Colorado Bob's.*

Colorado Bob's Ship of Fools was a pure dive in the Tower Grove South part of St. Louis. An actual dive. Not a 'dive bar'. Nothing pissed me off more than when a yuppie called an average or lesser frequented bar a 'dive'. I've come to realize that the meaning of the term 'dive bar' has experienced a rapid alteration over time, turning it into a false narrative. That's because normal people can't conceive how fucking dirty and decadent a real dive bar is. A tavern is not automatically a dive. Decent human beings don't go to dives. A true dive bar should be a detriment to the neighborhood it's in. Dives are volatile, disreputable, and unsavory. The drinking that takes place in a dive is not fun, it is not recreational.

It is a slow form of suicide. It is methodical and habitual.

The depth of depravity in a dive should be unfathomable to a normal contributing member of society. That is where I think the confusion comes into play with social drinkers erroneously characterizing middle-of-the-road bars as dives. They have no idea of the type of squalor and filth that inhabit real dive bars.

"Oh look, they have **PBR** cans! What a dive!"

If you don't walk in and are instantaneously overcome with an ominous expectation of being stabbed at any moment, it's probably not a dive. If you don't walk in to everyone glaring over their shoulder at you, it's probably not a dive. If there is a laminated menu, it's probably not a dive. If you can't buy condoms either from a machine in the bathroom, the bartender, or another patron, it's probably not a dive. If you can order a craft beer on tap, get the fuck out of here moron, as it's definitely not a dive. If they sell T-shirts with the bar's name written on it, it's probably not a dive. And if they call themselves a dive bar, they are not a dive bar. 'Dive' has to be one of the most overused words in the English lexicon, just behind 'love' and 'genius'.

I once took a girl to Tom's Bar & Grill in Central West End and she called it a dive. In a possible overreaction, I pledged to never see her ever again and we went Dutch on the tab. Tom's was nice. It was cozy, safe, and had upkeep. I loved Tom's, but it was nowhere near a dive bar.

When I first moved to St. Louis and heard the term misused several times, I thought maybe it had slightly different variations of the definition based on what part of the country you're in. I grew up in Northern Wisconsin where there were bars that sold meth in the backroom and people threw pool balls in fights. I once witnessed a guy walk into the bar, put a quarter in the jukebox, played a Hank Williams Jr. song, knocked a guy out cold clean off his bar stool, smoked a cigarette, and left... all without saying a word. The bartender didn't even intervene, just kept cleaning a pint glass. That was a Sunday afternoon. Now *that's* a dive bar.

However, the longer I lived in St. Louis the more degenerates I met, and I realized there was a plethora of true dives in the city. The definition was not geographically varied, millennials everywhere just loved ruining things by trying to evolve them and their meaning into what they thought was cool, but in actuality was just utter shit. Anyway. I digress. I drove over to Colorado Bob's and thus commenced the weirdest Sunday of my life.

13

As I walked into the infamous bar I instantly saw my friends Ian, Aaron, Sarah, Nick, and Shelley as well as two other girls I didn't know propping up the bar, half of them standing, half of them sitting. I hung out with this group rarely, for no particular reason other than our only common interest was drinking. They greeted me enthusiastically and I was promptly handed a shot of Fireball. I ordered a beer. Five minutes later I ordered another one. Sunday Funday was in full effect. What I liked about this group as a crew of drinkers was that there were no side conversations going on. It was always one collective conversation with quips, puns, and vulgarity, always ensuing laughter. They were a group of power drinkers. This Sunday Funday was not going to be a brisk picnic in the park with Frisbee throwing and finger sandwiches. This was get drunk or get ostracized. We stayed at Colorado Bob's for another drink and reconvened to the Soulard neighborhood where all the best power drinkers within the city limits gravitated on Sundays.

We walked into a bar called The Shanti and it was apparent the real drinkers were already in full swing the moment we walked through the door. Without even making it to the bartender to order a beer, a meth-fueled, bald-headed 40-year-old-ish ghoul approached us holding a large squash with things written all over it in Sharpie.

"HEY, SIGN MY SQUASH!"

"What the fuck is that for?" I asked.

"YOU GOTTA SIGN MY SQUASH, MAN!!! I FORGOT MY WIFE'S BIRTHDAY! SIGN MY SQUASH!"

Apparently, this meth-head had forgotten his wife's birthday and in an attempt to elicit her forgiveness/minimize the impending domestic assault he was having everyone within eyesight sign this squash as some sort of pseudo birthday card. I was bewildered but amused. This wasn't that uncommon a start for drinking on a Sunday in Soulard.

There were already a lot of signatures and cuss words written on the squash so I knew he wouldn't be able to distinguish anything that I wrote. So without him paying much attention I took the squash and wrote 'get a new husband' on it and handed it back to him.

"THANKS MAN! WHAT DID YOU WRITE?!"

"Happy Birthday."

We moved past the squash pusher and made it to the bar. The Shanti had a vibrant patio area with a lot of interesting decor and different seating arrangements, including an old boat. We approached the patio bar and I noticed a set of twins. They were not twins like you'd see in a Coors Light commercial, however. They were 50-year-old brothers with matching beards. There was an open stool next to them which I took as I ordered myself a drink.

The barmaid was uniquely beautiful in a scummy

kind of way. She had dyed raven black hair with bangs, a nose piercing, and several odd tattoos covering her sleeveless arms. She placed my beer bottle down and rather than going back to my group I started eavesdropping on the twins. They were apparently arguing about who was the smarter of the two.

"Bullshit! I'm 'bout 10 times smarter than you. Yew don't even got yer GED," Twin A said.

"That don't mean shit. I'm smarter than yew. Your dumbass can't even read. What's that sign say over there?" Twin B responded. Twin A started to squint at the sign for about a second before his brother continued, "IT SAYS HALF-OFF TAPS ON TUESDAY, DUMBASS!" For some reason this made Twin A concede the intelligence, or lack of, argument and he moved on to appearance.

"All right, yew might be smarter but I'm better lookin'."

"Bullshit! I've had like a hundred girlfriends… how many have you had? Like, none?"

At this point I was laughing to myself, looking to my right and into my shoulder so they would not acknowledge my amusement. These did not seem like the type of guys you want to catch you laughing at. I looked back over to our group. Sarah was taking a shot with squash guy's soon-to-be ex-wife. I then turned back to the twins. They were now talking about who was stronger. They decided to solve the debate logically by arm wrestling. They moved to a two-seat table nearby and locked hands and elbows. I decided to interject for amusement and in fairness to the sport of arm wrestling.

"You guys mind if I officiate? I want a nice clean fight here today gentlemen."

They both nodded in agreement and I checked for any wrist curling and clean grips. I then firmly grabbed the top of their interlocked hands and counted down from three… "annnnnnnd arm wrestle!"

snap

After a few seconds of struggle, I heard a grotesque popping sound and watched them both cease pressure immediately. Twin A's arm was lying limp on the table and he instantly went into shock. His brother literally broke his humerus in his upper arm from the pressure of the opposing forces and resulting torque. They were both frantic and Twin B started yelling for shots of whisky. He ordered three, two for his injured brother and one for himself. As his second priority, he told the scummy-yet-beautiful barmaid to call an ambulance. She brought over a rag filled with ice and told them someone was on the way to take him to the hospital.

No one from our group or at the other end of the bar in general knew what was taking place. I was excited to tell them. Within about 10 minutes the ambulance arrived. They sat him up on the gurney and wheeled him out of the bar as he raised his good arm in triumph as everyone in the bar cheered. His twin brother followed behind apologizing profusely.

Almost in the same exact instant they exited the bar, the place resumed normal activity. There was fierce Sunday drinking yet to be had.

Some of our group had moved into the actual indoor bar of The Shanti. I walked in and immediately saw Aaron coming out of the bathroom. He saw me, came over with a smirk on his face and shook my hand, leaving a dime bag of cocaine in it.

Typically, I would be against this form of recreational

abuse on a Sunday with work the following day, but I was already slightly drunk. And cocaine was great. I ducked into the bathroom, took out my pocketknife, and did two sizable bumps. I was in and out of that bathroom is under a minute. St. Louis is pretty far from Mexico, so I was surprised how good the cocaine was. Instantly I felt like I could break everyone's arm in the entire bar. I went up to a woman and attempted to talk to her.

"Hey," I said.

"Hey, I'm Analise," she said with a smile.

"How many 'N's is that spelled with?"

"One, why?"

"Do people call you Anal for short?"

"Fuck off."

Somehow Analise was impervious to my charm. Shortly after I was informed we were relocating to Beale on Broadway, yet another bar. I was idiotically still driving at this point and felt assured that the blow would give me the confidence and the concentration to make the quick drive downtown. As I sauntered outside to my car, there was a young attractive woman standing in front of it looking somewhat emotionally disheveled. We looked at each other for a few seconds. She had beautiful pure hazel eyes and dark black hair with a svelte figure. I was spellbound. She understood me to be the owner of the car as I got closer and informed me that she had hit it trying to park.

"Jesus woman. Where?"

"On the back-left part of the car, just barely. I don't see anything, but I felt like I needed to tell you."

"How long have you been standing there?"

"Half an hour."

"Well, I don't see anything. Looks fine to me. I'm

going to Beale on Broadway with my friends... want to join? I have illegal drugs. Also, you owe me. If you don't come, I might have to reappraise the damage. Could be expensive."

"You said there was no damage! How do I know you're not a serial killer?"

"You don't. That's why it's fun. Follow me there, I'll teach you how to park without hitting another vehicle."

She actually said okay. Less than 10 minutes later we were exchanging names and getting drinks. Beale on Broadway was a true dive—a blues bar just on the outskirt of downtown. It had a tented patio bar with a stage and an inside bar as well. Dan Aykroyd performed a song from *Blues Brothers* there once. Robert Plant also frequented the bar when he was in St. Louis while on tour. It was my favorite music venue in town despite the limited capacity of about 50 persons. I looked over to my group and saw the squash guy's wife again. I asked her where her squash was. She said it was in bed with her passed-out, tired excuse for a husband.

The girls name was Mandi. I asked if she wanted a bump. She said drugs were lame. Strike one. I asked if she'd ever done them. She said no. Strike two. I told her she was on thin ice. We moved past her devotion to D.A.R.E. and started talking about ourselves.

"So, what do you do for a living Chris?"

"I design drink coasters. What do you do?"

"Wait, seriously? That's a job?"

"Yeah, apparently."

"Like what kind of designs?"

"I do a lot with woodland creatures. People love them. So, what's your job?"

She did something that included a 9-to-5 schedule, I

don't exactly remember. I excused myself to the bathroom to do my last hit of coke before I gave the bag back to Aaron. I walked into a stall where I faced the toilet and took the bag out of my pocket. I started rustling with it and the knife to do another two bumps as the door opened. It was the manager. I quickly zipped the bag back up and pretended to start pissing. The urinal was open, and he heard the sound of the bag rustling, so the manager put two and two together and said, "Listen man, I don't care if you do it—I do it all the time—just don't fucking do it in here."

"Piss?"

"Very funny. Sounded like you were doing something else."

"I was checking my receipt for the drinks I just bought."

"Whatever man, don't get this bar in trouble."

In retrospect I should have offered him a line. He promptly left the bathroom and I very quietly and remorselessly did another two bumps off my pocketknife before going back out into the bar. I gave Aaron the bag subtly and informed him of the staff narc.

I went back to Mandi and instantly proposed a pair of shots. She obliged. We continued to drink and mingled with the group a bit. Sarah made out with squash guy's wife. I asked Mandi if she wanted to come back to my place. She obliged. It was possible this girl had never said no to anything in her entire life. Other than drugs, of course.

We arrived at my place around 9:00 pm and I made a couple drinks as she took in all the hoarder-like shit I had strewn around my apartment. She asked to see my coasters. I said I didn't use any. We eventually moved to the bed. I was horny to a large extent but unfortunately had contracted a grueling case of coke-dick. I could not get it up. Eventually the coke wore off and I passed out. The next morning, I woke up to a note that said,

Hey let me know if anything is wrong with your car.
Mandi. 314-574-8834

14

By itself, a hangover is a mild situational inconvenience and far from complaint worthy. Suck it up. Oh, you're hungover Sunday morning with an 18-hour date with the couch? Big whoop. Funnel some Pedialyte and eat a burrito. Fall asleep to a shitty Steven Seagal movie. Get over it. But pair a hangover with some sort of crippling responsibility or a place you need to be? Now that's a living hellhole. The Monday morning hangover at work is an apprehension-filled balloon waiting to pop. A snake pit of misery. With my weekly Monday meeting that morning I could not have slid in late undetected. Especially not with Officer Judy sitting to the left of me, keeping an internal time stamp of my arrivals each day. I contemplated calling in sick. I quickly dismissed the idea because our vacation and sick days were combined as what was commonly known as 'PTO'—personal time off. I wasn't going to waste a vacation day hungover in bed. I had to go in. The second I stood up I felt nauseous, but not nauseous enough to throw up. A hangover paradox. There was no conceivable way I was going to make it into work and survive a meeting in said state. I had a harrowing thought of sharing my 'weekend win'. I felt sicker. Hair of the dog would not work, but uppers could be another story. I threw on some clothes, walked out into the hallway, and knocked on my neighbor Christina's door. She possessed an Adderall prescription. I knew this because she had given me a few throughout the year while partying on our roof. She was luckily getting ready for work like a normal person and opened the door. In an unbecoming fashion I literally begged for a pill. Describing my predicament, I offered money, half-full bottles of alcohol, and her favorite meal that night. She laughed and went to her purse and procured me two four-hour pills. I gratefully hugged her and asked what I could give her in the return. "On the house," she said.

I showered and got properly dressed before taking the first pill with some water and a plain toasted bagel. Christina's pills had a slow release but there was a psychological effect already commencing that made me feel better and hopeful for the day. I made my walk into the office—13 women.

I got into the office relatively on time. Greg, having been there for 20 minutes already, was planted firmly in his chair reading his daily news articles. Of all websites to get his news from, he used the yahoo.com homepage simply because it was the set homepage of the computer when he first started.

"Why don't you just change the homepage to something better than Yahoo?"

"Can't."

"You literally can. It's a simple setting to change."

"I know how to change it. I'm great with computers. But this is what the company wants it to be, Christopher."

"Okay. How are you this morning?"

"Pretty chipper actually. The best feeling in the world

is coming into the bathroom and the seat is up and the water is blue. First go-around of the day... and the week!"

"I think you could benefit from a psychiatrist," I said.

"Saw one once. Court ordered. Clean bill of health. I actually helped him fix his computer."

The VP of Sales Strategy had a lot to do that morning so fortunately made the meeting go quickly and we completely skipped our wins. At this point the Adderall had started doing its job quite well. I was hit with a newfound energy and buoyancy.

I returned to my desk and checked my schedule for the day. I realized I had meeting with a new client that purchased our services the week before, a local locksmith and key copy business. They were looking to do local TV commercials and needed help with a 30-second spot. They would be in our conference room in 15 minutes to go over my ideas. Fuck. Ideas. This had been on my calendar for a week and circled in red to indicate its urgency. For the ensuing 15 minutes I became distracted and found myself on Sandra Bullock's Wikipedia page for reasons unknown.

Our receptionist walked over to my desk, "Chris, A-Plus Lock & Key Company are here to see you."

The owners were two out-of-shape grizzly looking men with impeccable gray mustaches and guts mimicking bowling balls. Their tucked-in, buttoned-up workman shirts emphasized their pregnancy bellies. I greeted them with firm handshakes, "Gentlemen. Chris Van Zandt." Based on their appearance I could have guessed their names in less than 10 attempts. Bob and Hank. I almost laughed on the spot. Bob started the meeting with his thoughts.

"So Chris, we have heard you are the guy with the *funny* ads. The memorable ones that stick in people's minds. We sell spare keys and help people when they are locked out, so we can't really push product. We just want people to think of us when they need these services. We were told comedy or a catchy jingle usually does the trick. And as we hate jingles, we were directed to you."

We had a contracted freelance musician that made jingles for us. I envied him, and truth be told I even tried a couple myself, but it never panned out. That asshole worked two hours a day from his home and made more money than any of us. I digress.

Hank eloquently piggy-backed off Bob's introduction, "So what do you have for us?"

Come on Adderall... turn some fucking wheels... spew some bullshit... spare keys... spare keys...?

"I was thinking a fake bachelor reality show."

"Excuse me?"

"Pardon Chris?" Bob and Hank replied in unison.

"Hear me out. The Bachelor and The Bachelorette are the two most watched reality shows right now. I just dated a girl who did a Bachelor fantasy draft with her friends. We make a commercial with a reality show called *My Spare Keys*. A bachelor is looking for a girl to take his spare keys as a romantic interest. We hire a few good-looking women and take 20–25 seconds with a comedy spoof and the last five–10 plugging your business. It's funny. People will remember it when they need a spare key. It has potential to go viral on the internet if we do it right."

Bob and Hank sat in silence for a few moments until they looked at each other and Bob said,

"That's fuckin' brilliant. How do we start?"

Crisis averted. I ended the meeting with a plan of

action to get the commercial scripted and produced and they were on their way. I came back to my desk and looked at the rest of the day. It was 10:45. I had a phone call at 3:00 pm with an IPA brewery looking for a commercial idea. I decided to take a two-hour lunch break and grab some greasy food. The Adderall was working, but I still needed to properly tend the hangover fermenting in my guts. The effects of Adderall were simply acting as a placeholder and disguising the booze flu with good feelings. Hangovers could not be cured, only managed and endured.

I walked over to Jack Patrick's for lunch. It was a beautiful hole-in-the-wall downtown joint with incredible pub food in a walkup window in the corner of the bar. I ordered a burger with fries and sat at the bar. I hadn't planned on drinking for a few days after the weekend bender I was coming off, but sitting at a bar drinking an ice water made me feel like a teetotaling fuckwad. I ordered a beer and turned my attention to the TV. It was a commercial for Michelob Ultra. Mich Ultra was marketed as a 'healthy beer' with very few calories and carbs compared to other brews. They considered themselves the healthiest beer option on the market. The commercial featured several fit, athletic, gorgeous-looking people with perfect bodies playing volleyball at the beach while drinking their product, all teeth, tits, and smiles. It emphasized that you can have rock hard abs and still drink beer. I fucking hated it. I hated everyone in the fucking commercial. Not out of jealousy, just out of sheer annoyance. How did these people all find each other? There was no way they are enjoying the beer-water, I thought to myself. My burger arrived and despite Adderall alleviating one's appetite I still managed to finish it without difficulty. I decided to have another beer as a palate cleanser. Valid reasoning. At Jack Patrick's bar there was a mirror facing the stools, spanning the entire length of the bar-back. I looked at myself. I looked like pure shit. Like wet, freshly laid unadulterated human shit. The drinking and drugs were inevitably taking a toll on my face and body. It did not discourage my decision to order another beer. I decided to try a Mich Ultra. I guess the commercial worked. I swallowed my second Adderall pill with the first sip and instantly had an idea for my IPA client meeting later.

***

As usual, Greg did not miss a beat when I returned from lunch. "Lunch break is typically an hour, Christopher."

"Greg, have you ever thought of getting a new job? You hate this place. And I'm getting kind of sick of you."

"Yeah, but I have a pension. Do you know how rare that is nowadays? If I don't have any more out-of-wedlock kids I'm taking the early pension at 50 and leaving. I will just shag golf balls at Tower Tee for walking around money. Why do you smell of beer?"

My meeting was a conference call with the married owners of Mad Dog Brewery, and they were launching a new Indian Pale Ale. They purchased a few local commercial spots and wanted, in their own words, 'an on-the-edge-funny' commercial. Luckily, I was feeling very on-the-edge-funny after my 32 ounces of beer and 20 milligrams of Adderall.

"Kenny, Jolene—thanks for the opportunity," I said into the phone's mic, "I believe I have an idea. Have you seen the Mich Ultra commercial where all these ridiculously good-looking young people are playing volleyball on the beach and drinking bottles of Mich Ultra?"

"Yeah, I believe so," Jolene answered.

"Well, I think that commercial is inherently stupid," I said, "I'm not looking for a beer to drink while I go whitewater kayaking down a Colorado river. And if I am, I'm not choosing one that tastes like the piss of a well-hydrated cat. Cheeseburgers and pizza aren't two of the most frequently ordered restaurant items of all time because they are the healthiest thing on the menu. No one goes out of their way to procure the city's best *apple*. IPA beers are far from light in calories or carbs, which is as they should be. People drink beer because they want the effects of alcohol that make them feel good and because the taste is good. You two make beer that taste great, I've tried it. Please forgive me if I don't drink your beer while paragliding over the alps. With that being said, I think we should get a bunch of normal-looking, out-of-shape people attempting extreme sports while drinking an unnamed 'Ultra-Light Beer' similar to the Mich Ultra commercial, but not enough to get sued by them. Picture an overweight gentleman, five feet off the ground, rock climbing. He cracks open a cold one and his face recoils in taste bud horror and he goes back to trying to climb. He then realizes the activity is asinine and goes to the bar and orders your IPA with a smile on his face as we see him enjoying a large gulp. This is repeated with other out-of-shape, everyday people attempting other pointless extreme activities – parkour, bungee jumping, kiteboarding, that sort of thing. They all give up, toss the cat piss over their shoulder, and we cut to them walking into your brewery for this delicious IPA. At the end of the commercial everyone previously shown is found hanging out together having the fucking time of their lives—pardon my language—at your brewery drinking IPA and you deliver your tagline. 'Drink Beer Because it Tastes Good. Our Beer Tastes Good'."

Speechless. I imagined them jumping down the phone line to kiss me, maybe a little tug job from the wife. They were very pleased, as was I. We made a plan of action from there. Two little pills transformed quite possibly the worst Monday in my adult life into one of the most successful. Around quitting time, the second pill wore off, but I didn't care. I felt great.

15

As that summer wore on, I grew out my hair. It was noticeably long for a guy. God or maybe evolution or heredities or abiogenesis or some other propositional belief had blessed me with beautiful, curly, luscious hair. Knowing I possessed this inimitable head of silk salad, I occasionally grew it long. It would have been a crime against humanity if I didn't. A few years back I had grown it especially long and reluctantly cut it short too soon. Very similar to when Michael Jordan quit the NBA to go play minor league baseball. A disgraceful mistake. As I grew it out again, I was at a bit of an awkward stage. It had outgrown the 'Cool yet still somewhat professional Bradley Cooper/Matthew McConaughey' stage but was not quite in the 'Shoulder-length, nonchalant surfer' stage yet. I was currently in what I identified as the 'Disgusting vagrant' stage.

The biggest misconception about guys with long hair was that they were lethargic. Like when my bosses called me 'lazy' or 'unmotivated' or 'on thin ice' all because I had long hair. But it required a large amount of upkeep unbeknownst to them. So one weeknight I decided to step my hair product game up in order to circumvent the split-ends, frizz, and dryness. I did some research while also making friends in an online long hair forum for men. I had all the answers I needed plus a couple confusing yet enticing private messages from L0nghairfu©ker69. I headed to Walgreens.

I was looking for an argan oil shampoo and conditioner with a type of refining cream. What was most interesting about my search in this St. Louis Walgreens was that the hair care aisle was patently racially segregated. On the right-hand side of the aisle all the hair care products had pictures of good-looking black people on them and on the left they all had photos of good-looking white people on them. I understood the genetic differences in hair texture between the two, so I was not offended by this apparent apartheid. I moved on from this observation and turned my attention to the left-hand side of the aisle, despite my longtime curiosity of how afros worked.

After 45 minutes of reading labels and Googling product reviews on my phone, I came to a steadfast decision that I felt good about.

OGX Hydrate + Repair Argan Oil of Morocco Extra Strength Shampoo & Conditioner: Repair the damage of over-styled brittle hair with this extra powerful blend of argan oil from Morocco to help mend and hydrate while silk proteins and strengthen tresses to give your hair a second chance at soft, seductive silky perfection.

I would have bought just about anything with the word 'silky' on the packaging.

Like most people, I was a big fan of all that Walgreens had to offer so I continue to shop around aimlessly. My interest piqued in the condom aisle. I was staring at all the different types and brands. I saw words like 'thintensity', 'ecstasy', 'ultra-ribbed', and 'extended pleasure'. I did not know what any of these things meant but I was intrigued. I contemplated buying some, even though I still had that three-pack leftover from last year. At that moment a random lady in the aisle walked by and noticed my Argan Oil of Morocco shampoo and conditioner.

She stopped, looked at me, and had the audacity to utter, "Oh, does your lady like that stuff too?!"

What the fuck do you mean, 'Does my lady like that stuff too?' I thought. It's for me you fucking idiot. *Look at my hair.* You think I use some shitty 2-in-1 made by a deodorant company? I looked at her in outright disgust and responded with, "Hell no, this is for me," as I grabbed a handful of my hair as if to put it in her face and be like, 'Look at this you stupid bitch'. She laughed as I walked away appalled.

Two minutes later I passed by the woman again. This time I was in front of all the different types of mouthwash, which was also captivating but not as much as the condoms. She quickly glanced at me and then to no one in particular, she repeated my response, "HA HA! Hell no, this is for me – ha ha ha."

At this point I had never been more offended in my entire life. I could honestly say I was officially a victim of gender discrimination. I finally knew what women in several conservative communities across Saudi Arabia and Pakistan were going through when they were forbidden to drive a vehicle or go out in public without a male chaperone. It was almost a perfect analogy for what I experienced.

I was so sick of the gender stereotypes and all the multifarious sexist prejudices occurring. ON BOTH SIDES. What was wrong with men wanting to revitalize their hair? Why were all the most famous tyrannical dictators men? Why didn't men get paid maternity leave?

Where were all the female computer hackers? How come when my ex-girlfriend slept over at my place, she could wear my clothes to bed but when I stayed at her place it was considered 'super-fucking-weird' to wear her clothes to bed? How come women could look sexy drinking fun, fruity cocktails but when men did it, we looked 'ass-puckeringly gay'? All these things bothered me, on both sides, because I was into equality. Was I hero because I bought nice hair care products in the face of adversity? Maybe, yeah. Hero actually sounds pretty fitting. But I digress.

About two weeks later I cut my hair short.

16

To commemorate my new haircut I decided to go out on Saturday night. I wanted to meet women now that I looked employed again. I appeared to have outdrank my normal drinking circle around that time so I had to go deep into the friend roster to find a partner in crime. Literally. I felt like breaking laws. I texted my friend Otto who lived in Soulard. Otto was a reformed alcoholic with bisexual tendencies. At about five-foot-six with bright red fiery hair and freckles, he was about as close to a living, breathing leprechaun you would ever see within city limits. But he made me laugh regularly. Otto was genuinely funny in social groups, even more so sober. It was 8:30 pm so naturally he was already at a local Soulard patio bar. After a brief back-and-forth of texts I found my way over to meet him and his friends.

As I walked in Otto immediately greeted me in his usual chipper disposition. "Let's get you a drink, buddy boy!" We approached the bar and he ordered me a beer and he ordered himself... a milk. A literal single serving carton of milk. They brought him one after a few minutes. Like a secret menu item that no one other than Otto would ever order. He opened his milk and took a sip. "Ahhh, that's the good stuff! Nothing like an ice-cold milk after a long hard day. Am I right or am I right, Chris? You know I'm right." Otto was one of my favorite wingmen of all-time. He was a self-described bisexual, but he definitely came off as a bit gay in his mannerisms. When I say he came off a 'bit gay' I mean he came off very gay, but he liked to fuck women as well, so he made his flamboyancy as adjustable as a volume dial. He knew I liked meeting women at the bars and was very good at approaching groups, because again, at 5'6" and scorching hot red hair, he was adorable and always the least threatening person in the room. As we took a lap of the bar, he started going up to girls, offering his milk, and asking if they wanted a drink, telling them they had weak bones. "Come on girls, it does the body good! I want you all to grow up to be strong and healthy women." Although no one drank the milk, they all thought he was pretty funny.

With Otto's milk schtick we eventually met a group of girls, including one named Emma who I liked straightaway. She had beautiful brown eyes and large breasts. I noticed these qualities in reverse order. Anyone who laughs at a guy drinking a school-lunch-sized milk carton at a bar probably had a great sense of humor and she solidified this theory. I was enjoying talking to her. At some point in our conversation Otto brilliantly interjected himself and hammed up his gay side. It was obvious he preferred to fuck men on this night, at least as far as Emma was concerned.

As we joked around a bit more, Otto's wingman capabilities grew stronger, like he was a mustachioed plumber named Mario who had just encountered a patch of mushrooms. He always knew how to steer the conversation to sex in one way or another. He complimented her breasts and asked to feel them. Assuming he was in fact gay, Emma let him without question. Otto moved behind and encircled her body with his hands, taking his time to admire their pendulous weight and shapeliness while muttering smut into her ear and making her laugh. This went on for a good 10 seconds. At this moment it was abundantly clear why I hung out with him. He said thank you after feeling her up and left us to talk some more. After a couple more drinks, Emma and I left together. Her place was within walking distance nearby. Pretty soon we were sitting in her kitchen, drinking and talking until her roommate came home. Along with her roommate was her very intoxicated asshole boyfriend. They sat in the kitchen for a bit with us and it was apparent they had a rough night domestically. The wasted boyfriend kept trying to high-five me while asking, "wasssssup brotha?" The roommate seemed sober and unamused. The drunk poured himself straight vodka into a dirty coffee cup from the sink and went and sat in the living room. Emma proceeded to tell me they were beginning to get the impression he was an alcoholic. I responded apathetically.

"Probably."

We eventually moved to Emma's room and got into her bed, violently flirting. In an attempt to feel her provocative protuberances myself, I told her Otto slept with women. "So you're going to let my friend fondle your boobs half a minute after meeting him, but I am in your bed and staying the night with you and I can't? What kind of erratic logic is that?"

I felt her tits. They were super nice. Thanks Otto.

She didn't want to have sex because she had morals

or something and so we eventually fell asleep. In the morning she asked to grab breakfast, but I told her I had a 10:00 am tee time. Every guy had a 10:00 am tee time the next morning. Even those who didn't play golf. I told her I would call her soon. I walked out the door and realized she never even gave me her number. Oh well. At least I knew where she lived.

17

An event I had been looking forward to for an unhealthy amount of time had finally arrived. A college wedding back in Nashville, Tennessee. A rarity in wedding invites, I was to everyone's surprise platonic friends with the bride-to-be. She was best friends with my ex-girlfriend from college. I was obviously no longer dating my college sweetheart at this time but the bride, Kaylee, was a lovely human being so we remained friends, even after the tumultuous breakup.

She was marrying the type of dude you should hate with envy but genuinely like because he's irritatingly quite lovely. His background was as follows: played college quarterback at Michigan, MBA from Columbia, then quit his job on Wall Street to start a wildly successful whiskey distillery. He was actually the backup QB at Michigan, which made him even more likable. Backup quarterback is, in my opinion, the best position in all of sports. To top off the resumé, the quarterback he was behind on the depth chart? Grayson Flynn, the highly touted, first-round NFL draft pick who was considered the best quarterback in college football in his senior year. To most people's delight Grayson was a groomsman at the wedding.

It was a beautiful 103-degree day in Nashville, perfect for sweating uncontrollably through a cheap polyester H&M suit. The ceremony was fabulous... or whatever. A girl next to me accused me of crying during the vows. I told her it was just my allergies. They sometimes acted up when I got really emotional.

The reception was held in a rustic barn deep in the country, beautifully constructed with a lustrous and highly polished wood finish throughout. It was the kind of barn I'd think baby Jesus was born in if his family came from money. They had an open bar stocking Tennessee whiskey. My very imprecise strategy as a single guy at wedding receptions had always been to drink until something or someone suggested itself, especially if I didn't know anyone there. That typically meant drink until I saw an attractive girl to make a fool of myself in front of. It was getting old. And frankly, I didn't care about chasing the glamourous and exotic tail at this reception. I wanted to talk to the gorgeous Grayson Flynn. I had always felt like an unaccredited counterfeit type of journalist, so this was the time to prove that insignificant self-proclaimed label. This was a very small ceremony, 100 people tops, so I knew I had a unique opportunity.

I finally saw an opening and made my move.

"Hey bud, what's up... Chris," I said as I offered a firm yet delicate handshake. Grayson wasn't rude but he wasn't engaging either. He had just finished warming the bench in St. Louis for the Rams before they relocated to Los Angeles, so I had common ground. "So what did you think of that shithole St. Louis?" I asked.

"It wasn't that bad," he articulately responded.

I asked him a couple more questions and said I liked

his last interview on *The Dan Patrick Show*. I did this without trying to sound like I wanted to give him a reach-around. With a continued lack of effervescence in his responses, I promptly left him alone. It seemed he had little interest in talking to a Division II college football dropout such as myself. He was the 14th overall pick in the NFL draft, after all. Supercilious prick.

The wedding reception ended and there was a giant party bus to take all the fun young people out on Broadway to a private upstairs bar. Apparently this was a yearly membership type of place, and not widely promoted... kind of a hidden secret. So tourists and squares weren't allowed. But you know who was allowed? Gay guys. As they should be. I'm a fan of the gay community, but more on that later. We arrived and as far as I was told, after only being there a mere five minutes two gay gentlemen had recognized Grayson and started talking, ostensibly hitting on him. For whatever reason, whether it was uncomfortable for him or possibly just annoying because people bothered him at bars a lot, he excused himself and came and stood on the other side of me, like I was some sort of homosexual repellent. A guy from the wedding party I was talking to earlier came up to my other side and said, "So I guess those faggots were hitting on Grayson. We are going to beat the shit out of them."

"Cool, dude," I replied in a toneless lie... because that was *not* cool.

Now I am in no way insinuating that Flynn was homophobic, although he had previous reported instances in the media of being so. But a few of the other guys at the wedding? Clearly. It's very possible Grayson was just annoyed, and it had nothing to do with the fact they were gay. I was not famous, despite my meteoric rise as a mid-level local advertising executive, so I could not comprehend what it was like to be bothered every time I graced the public with my presence.

But how do you not love the gays? As a heterosexual male I thanked God for the existence of gay men every day of my life. First off, they are incredibly complimentary. If I was ever struck with a feeling of low self-esteem I would just stroll into a gay bar. I was so fuckable! I was the number one overall pick in the Gay Bar draft, not the embarrassing 14th pick. I had never felt so good about myself than when I'm in a gay bar. Maybe Greg had a point.

Secondly and more importantly, they take themselves out of the running in the race for vaginal procurement.

Traditionally, gay fellows are well-groomed, good-looking, in-shape dudes who would plow through pussy like a cornfield if they were straight. That is a wild marginalization of the gay community but let's continue with that typecast for the sake of the argument. The fact that these fit and attractive men fuck each other instead of beautiful women is amazing and quite possibly the greatest benefaction to the straight man of all time. You could go as far as to say that I would have never been laid if not for gay guys. No other context necessary, just quote that sentence. I tried to coerce my good-looking friends into being gay all the time.

"Come on dude, just try it out! Come on out of the closet! Have you ever tried it? No? Well, then how do you know you're not gay? Be gay, be yourself!" Everyone knows that being gay is a choice and I thank the altruistic men who have made that decision.

Nonetheless, it's safe to assume that Grayson had

never had a problem getting women. He was married to a stunningly gorgeous three-time LPGA major tournament winner, but me, I thank the gays for their service. But not lesbians though. Fuck lesbians.

At any rate, Grayson came and stood next to me while this altercation was brewing, and I never passed up an opportunity to be a troll. I didn't care if you were famous or smarter than me, I was going to make jokes at your expense. If you can't take a joke, fuck you. You want to be treated like a regular guy and not a celebrity? Okay, well I'm going to shame you for boisterous gay men hitting on you, because it's funny to me that it bothers you.

I turned to Grayson and with a smug grin on my face said, "So I hear the boys really like ya, what are you doing standing next to me? Playing hard to get? Go close the deal." Grayson, who was very drunk at this point and somewhere around 4 inches taller and forty pounds heavier than me, looked down and replied with,

"Are you trying to get your ass kicked?"

"I don't think so," I said.

Grayson then asks, "Where are you from man?"

"Wisconsin," I answered truthfully.

"Well, where I'm from you get your ass kicked for saying shit like that."

Being quick-witted and knowledgeable of useless facts can be both a privilege and a curse, and in this instance it was more of a curse.

"But aren't you from Ohio?" I retorted with a laugh.

It was an involuntary reaction and one I immediately regretted. But seriously, no one gets their ass kicked in *Ohio*. Grayson slammed down his drink like it was a maximizing muscle-gaining protein shake after his workout and got in my face. It made a bit of a scene so Matt, the groom, came over almost instantaneously and moved Grayson away from me, and while chuckling, he said, "Dude, leave Chris alone." He turned to me and said, "Sorry man, he's wasted. And he's been fighting with his wife all night. Not in a great mood." I stayed as far away from Grayson as possible for the rest of the party. I actually ended up going home with one of the gay fellers. I was *their* backup QB. Just kidding. But they didn't get beat up or anything. It was just textbook brainless bar drama. Guys peacocking without anything happening. What a tease.

After a few somber goodbyes in the hotel lobby the next morning, I beamed the entire five-hour drive back to St. Louis, pleased with my newest addition to my ongoing collection of debauched drinking stories.

Congrats to Kaylee and Matt. I hope they enjoyed the matching stainless steel toilet brush and garbage can I bought them on their registry.

18

Late that summer I began talking to a new woman named Hannah. We met in line for a drink at a Billy Joel concert. She seemed more like a 'come over and hang out' type of girl and not a 'dinner in public' woman. So that is what I suggested. She agreed and invited me over to smoke weed. I smoked weed often enough but not habitually, and I always smoked either too little or too much. I never mastered the sweet spot. I arrived at her apartment in the DeMun neighborhood and was instructed to climb up the fire escape to get in. I rarely questioned the commands of women.

I arrived at the back door and was greeted by her mutt, Frank. I loved Frank. He was a good boy. And people names for dogs are always hilarious. Eventually Hannah and I cozied up on her couch and took multiple hits from her psychedelic-looking glass pipe. She poured me some wine and put on a sitcom called *Broad City*, a show about two girls navigating life in NYC. It was well-written and funny. We were on-and-off conversing as we watched the show and taking hits until we were full-on making out. It was at about that point that I became intensely high. Arguably too high for the setting—once again I had cruised right through the sweet spot and was picking up speed on the other side.

We became handsy. With her guidance, she introduced me to her breasts. I felt them in an exploratory manner and concluded that they were wonderful, yet she would not let my hands wander anywhere else. She also was not interested in going anywhere near my nether regions despite my unmistakable boner. When most guys are hard but the girl does not notice or care, we start to wave it around like it's a lightsaber operated by pelvic thrusts. In these scenarios the dick emulates a dog watching someone eat. Look at me. I'm here. I'm hungry. Hey. I want some. Have you noticed me yet? *I'm down here.* Look at how friendly and patient I am. Hi. HEY! WOOF WOOF?!

It became obvious she was not interested in anything other than kissing and second-base action. Why did I get keep inadvertently hooking-up with horny purity pledgers? She just kept making out and letting me feel her boobs endlessly. Because of this, my weird weed-brain started to conjure up thoughts about what it would be like to have dicks for fingers. I thought it would solve everything in this scenario. She gets what she wants. I get what I want. How crazy would dick fingers be? There were a lot of pros and cons my brain tried to comprehend. It would completely change the formal handshake. Would it still be cordial and professional? Or a type of foreplay? Would you piss like Spider-Man? Would they be flaccid most of the time? That would not be great for dexterity purposes. I eventually snapped out of it and stopped thinking about fingers as dicks. We stopped making out and at that point most of my stoned attention shifted to Frank, the good boy. After a few more episodes of female life in NYC and a bit more wine,

I went home. She told me to text her to hang out again.

I texted her the next night. For a few days we exchanged routine messages back and forth; there was very little chemistry. But I really liked her dog Frank. And her weed. I wanted to go back over there. I was also curious what Ilana and Abbi from *Broad City* were getting themselves into. We made plans for the following week.

The day we were supposed to hang out arrived and Hannah cancelled guilt-free. I replied asking when she wanted to reschedule. In a cruel display of ambiguity, she said she didn't know but hopefully soon. That frustrated me, but I wanted to seem like it didn't. I'm a cool guy, I thought. I have six other 'Hannah's' in my phone as we speak. I don't need you. So in response I typed out, *Welp… the ball is in your court*

Send.

Five seconds went by. Then 10. And then 20. I then actually comprehended what I had just texted. Wait – no, fuck. That is a stupid text. Come back. Shit. I just stared at the words on the screen for about 30 seconds. "Welp, the ball is in your court?!" I yelled out in my apartment alone. That is the single dumbest thing a guy has ever texted a girl in the history of cell phones. I had literally never used the word 'welp' in my entire life, either verbally or in a text. And who tells a girl the ball is in their court? That is not cool, Chris – in fact it's fucking lame.

She never texted back. I didn't blame her. I was so fucking bad at being single.

19

Walking to work that Friday I only saw a measly three women that I liked. I got to work and checked the *Business Insider* online journal. Trump. The Dow tumbling. Elon Musk smoking weed. More Trump. The #MeToo movement. It was the same thing every day. As I was reading an article about Blink-182's Tom DeLonge joining forces with former Pentagon officials to prove aliens were real, I got an unexpected text from my Canadian friend Big Dick Brad. We called him Big Dick Brad because his name was Brad and he had a large penis. He was living a few hours away in Illinois for a new corporate job and came to St. Louis sporadically for weekends of drinking and debauchery.

Anything going on in the Lou this weekend?

There wasn't, but I told him to come anyway. Brad was a great addition to my night life. He was 6'5" and had the face of Robert Pattison. Women surrounded him like flies on fresh shit. He was the only friend I'd ever had where *women* were constantly approaching *him*. The antithesis of the dating world. He got in around 7:00 pm that evening. BDB, my friend Bill, and I started having beers at my apartment.

After what seemed like a 30-pack between the three

of us, we decided to take our talents to The Dubliner located several blocks down Washington Avenue. The Dubliner was a two-level, multi-bar Irish pub and restaurant with a small stage for live music every weekend. For a long time it was the most revered downtown bar. At any given time you could find a group of bikers, a group of hipsters, and a group of lawyers all sitting within a table of one another. I thought it had the perfect amalgam of a bar: good enough to be an end-of-the-night destination but not nice enough to attract douchebags and stuck-up women. We arrived in a perfect well-oiled alcoholic state. We had energy but were coherent—sharp, almost. At some point in the night I found myself talking to a lady, probably about her goals and dreams. I failed to listen, but I had the look of someone who was listening intently. I only managed to get her number as she had morals or whatever and I went back over to Brad and Bill who were chatting up a pair of healthy-looking females. I entered the conversation as a fifth wheel and was indirectly introduced as Brad yelled, "Chris!" for all to hear.

"So how do you guys all know each other?" asked Heather, one of the girls.

"Human trafficking. We met on the dark web," I said.

"That's not funny."

"Yeah, I know."

Brad had told Heather and her friend Ally that we were all professional hockey players, currently in the AHL and hoping to make the St. Louis Blues NHL roster. This was a weirdly cerebral lie as preseason camp started the following week. The conversation was short-lived as Brad told me we were all going back to my place. Great. Maybe one couple or both would let me watch I thought to myself sarcastically. But miraculously as we were walking back to my apartment Bill received a call from his long-distance girlfriend. It was like she had a sixth sense when he was about to cheat. It was actually very impressive. Bill stayed back and dealt with the phone call, clearly arguing with his better half. I began unknowingly and unintentionally swooping in on Heather, the girl that was previously interested in Bill at the bar. She had very little patience and had already forgotten that Bill was even a person let alone a person she had just spent 45 minutes talking to. I was very steadfast that I would not hijack my friend's apple. She said he clearly had a girlfriend. "I want you", she muttered in a sad puppy voice. I decided at that point Bill didn't deserve her. We started making out as Brad and Ally began cheering. We got back to my place and started assuming positions. I took Heather into my bedroom. Bill stumbled in late and went immediately to the couch, patently pissed off at his girlfriend. I don't think he cared I took Heather from him, he just wanted to go to sleep. Brad blew up my air mattress and began walking around my apartment in an attempt to find a somewhat private area to put it in. He first tried the bathroom, but it wouldn't fit. Then the kitchen floor area, but it also wouldn't fit. Hallway entrance? Wouldn't fit there either. He finally dropped the mattress in the middle of the living room, the only available space for the queen-size thing. Ally looked at Bill on the couch and irritably said, "Can we get some fucking privacy?" Without even opening his eyes, Bill responded forcefully, "WHERE THE FUCK DO YOU WANT ME TO GO YOU DUMB BITCH?"

"Your friend is rude," she said to Brad.

"Yeah, he's a pretty ornery person usually," Brad comically said loud enough for Bill to hear.

Back in my room, Heather fell asleep immediately after sex. I couldn't sleep. As I laid there, wide awake and in silence, she farted. It didn't smell healthy. I thought about talking to her about it in the morning but ultimately decided against it.

The next morning as we all started getting up, Heather asked me for a ride to her brother's house where she apparently lived. If the toxic fart wasn't enough of a red flag on deciding whether or not to see her again, living with her male sibling as an adult certainly solidified the decision. But we were outstanding young gentlemen, so we gave them a ride. I made Brad drive because I was a terrible friend and host.

Brad had a used BMW SUV that fell in line with the pro hockey lie fairly well. His radio was broken at the time, but he didn't mention this. Ally sat in the front with Brad while Heather sat in between Bill and me in the back. Brad flourished in awkward situations, always finding a way to augment the awkwardness in way to entertain himself and in this instance Bill and me. "You girls made some huge mistakes last night. You don't even know us."

"I broke my heel last night!" Heather said in reply from the back.

"I wouldn't let my dog wear those shoes," Brad quickly retorted. Ally interjected to ease the tension.

"Okay, you guys are being kind of mean. How about we turn on some music? What kind of music do you like?"

"NOTHING! NO MUSIC! I HAVE A LOT OF FUNNY THINGS TO SAY AND YOU ARE GOING

TO SIT THERE AND LISTEN TO THEM," Brad screamed.

We arrived at Heather's brothers' house in Bumfuck, Illinois. After a detached goodbye, Brad rolled down his window and started yelling, "WALK OF SHAME! WALK OF SHAAAAAAAME!"

Suffice it to say we never saw Ally or Heather again.

20

To keep myself grounded, I liked to hang out with blue-collar guys once in a while—no big deal. I would usually meet them at a dive bar for a few buckets of beer. I decided to meet my friend Austin at The Dry Dock, a seedy joint out in the county. I saw 11 women on my walk to work I wanted to sleep with that morning. Austin was a truck driver for an alcohol distributor. As we drank our beers in harmony, we started swapping stories. He began telling me what he referred to as his 'tales of the road'. He first explained to me what a 'Lot Lizard' was. Turns out it's not a reptile and is actually a member of the human species. He defined them as trashy female prostitutes who frequented truck-stop parking lots and rest areas at night to solicit their services. Some of the lot lizards even used their own personal CB radios to advertise their raw materials. Innovative. They were also referred to as pavement princesses or sleeper leapers. I was intrigued.

He then proceeded to tell me the first time he discovered what secret code gay truck drivers would use to identify other gay drivers. Since the straight truckers had lot lizards to appease their carnal urges, the gay truck drivers quickly deciphered that they too needed to figure out a form of sexual gratification when on the road. However, much like being a professional football player or a soldier in the military, outing yourself could sometimes do more harm than good. It had the potential to make their job very uncomfortable, not to mention the inevitable marginalization and ostracism they would endure. So they needed a secret code to find others like them. Austin told me the story of when he learned this fascinating factoid. He had a strong southern accent when speaking. "So, we're at the truck stop, congregatin' and whatnot, and this guy comes up to me and he says, 'Hey good buddy'. So I say, 'Well, hey there feller. How are ya?' And this dude just fuckin' walks away. How goddamn rude is that? I turned to another driver I was talkin' to like, 'man I kinda want to kick that guy's ass'. And then he asked if I knew what 'Good Buddy' meant. I said no, what the hell's it mean? Well, get this, he tells me that 'Good Buddy' is code for him bein' a queer and he's tryin' to sniff out other queers to buttfuck or whatever. Ever since that day I'll notice on the breaker some fag tryin' to get some, like, "Hey there, this is Carl I'm on interstate 55 headin' north about to hit up exit 198 and I'm lookin' for a good buddy. Any good buddies out there? Over." As I was laughing, I remembered why I hung out with Austin. He continued, "Whatever man. Don't bother me none. The way I look at it, if them fags want to fuck each other it's just more pussy for me."

"How gracious of you," I said.

There was a sandwich shop in downtown St. Louis called Good Buddy's that I never looked at the same after that.

21

For several months a co-worker of mine—David the accountant—relentlessly tried to get me to go out drinking with him. David was a very softly spoken albeit bland nice guy. He had recently gone through a messy divorce at 45 years of age and was looking to get back 'out there'. I was one of the only single socialites that he knew. I liked David in the way you like your mail carrier. Simple nod, maybe a wave and a thank you for your service, but I'm not inviting you in to have a drink or play with my kids. He was just someone who existed. No one in the history of the world had ever thrown a party and said, "Oh man, we gotta get David to come!" He was your quintessential suburban dad—classic pastel-colored button up long sleeve tucked into stain-defending khakis with leather loafers. On Fridays he wore silly screen-printed dress socks to establish his 'wacky' personality.

I always found a way to avoid his wingman advances, as he was just too nice to say no to directly. I felt obligated to have a believable lie to tell him to avoid hurting his already mangled feelings that his ex-wife emotionally eviscerated before throwing him into her piping hot witch's cauldron. But when someone persists hard enough and long enough, it becomes more and more difficult to circumvent. I eventually caved and told David I would grab drinks with him in an attempt to meet women.

It was a Wednesday night and David choose a bar called Mike Talaynas Jukebox Restaurant. It was the type of bar a middle-aged divorcee would choose based on a Google search of 'hip bars to pick up women'. From the ceiling hung dozens of sparkling disco balls—115 to be exact. The walls were covered with mirrors and neon lights. In line with the rest of the decor there was of course a dance floor.

I told David I would meet him around 7:00 pm. I arrive promptly on time and to no surprise he was already there, eager to commence on a night out to meet a woman. Back on the frontline almost 20 years since he had last done so. Walking into Mike Talaynas I expected to see him skulking at the bar, elbows out, head down, sipping his drink through a red straw. I would come in like Ryan Gosling to his Steve Carell in the comedy *Crazy, Stupid, Love*. As far as I knew David had a lot of nice qualities as a human being, but none of these attracted women in a place like Talaynas. Those qualities were superlatives at local community churches and small-town bingo halls, but they came up short in loud dance clubs. I braced myself for the next couple hours of dejection and glumness ahead up until the moment I spotted David.

"Chris's here! Hey guys, my friend Chris is here! Let's do some shots!" David yelled this to people sitting next to him at the bar as he leapt out of his stool to greet me. "Chris, you want to do some shots? Let's do some shots!" I had no idea what I had just encountered. I think someone must have slipped him an upper. Maybe it was his first time trying caffeine. I was confused. This was not the David I had worked with for two years. We went over to the bar and he ordered us shots... of vodka. I felt like I was having a weird dream.

Yeah, so I was at Talaynas and our account David was there? We did shots of vodka together. He kept talking about getting some pussy.

After a shot of Russia's finest I ordered a beer and as per David's request we went to the edge of the dance floor and leaned on a standing-height table. To the right of us were two attractive Asian women. David leaned in and whispered, "Ya know Chris, I've always wanted to sleep with an Asian girl but I've never done it!" His whisper turned into a loud declarative statement towards the end of the sentence.

"Maybe you should go tell them that; I don't think they heard you properly," I retorted.

"Maybe I will!" he said enthusiastically. Suddenly David was talking to the two Asian women.

"Hey girls! Isn't this place awesome?!"

I couldn't tell if he was bombing or killing it. He ended up talking to them for several minutes, completely unmindful to the fact I was there. He didn't even bother to introduce me. What an asshole this guy was. He eventually came back to my side and started chatting with me again. He had a permanent grin across his face paired with a constant foot tapping along to the music, like a nervous tick that wouldn't go away. He seemed happier than anyone I had ever seen in my entire life. I went to grab another drink and when I returned to the dance floor I had to stop and squint in disbelief.

David was dancing in between the two Asian women, fist pumping and enthusiastically grinding. He saw me approach, looked at me, and yelled, "THIS IS MY ELEMENT!"

David was now my favorite drinking partner as well as my spirit animal. I stayed for another drink after that one, which was mostly spent standing alone in astonishment watching David operate around the entire bar talking to anyone and everyone who would listen, all with that stupid smile on his face. When I told him I was leaving he didn't seem to care. He hugged me and thanked me for coming and went back to dancing. Never judge a book by their boring cover.

David called in sick the next morning.

22

It was Saturday night and a few friends and I decided to go to Molly's in Soulard, an extremely crowded patio bar stuffed full of younger people milling around like a herd of thirsty sheep. Since Greg only lived a few blocks away I texted him a last-minute invite. Not only did he accept and beat us to the bar, he was already wildly drunk when we got there. He spent all day drinking at the Lemp Mansion by himself, mingling with strangers (Greg had a weird fondness for the Lemp Mansion bar and restaurant and would often go there on his own). As we arrived he waved us over and threw his credit card on the bar. He informed the bartender that he would cover all our drinks but to only let us order buckets of domestic beer. This monetary gesture confused me because the week prior I had asked Greg to grab a burger after work and he said he could not afford one and was going to eat something at home. As the night grew noisier Greg took his shirt off. He also began lifting bar stools over his head, claiming it was the Stanley Cup and that it "felt great to be a champion." He eventually found his way to the dance floor to give yet more amusement to the group.

Suddenly I felt a tap on my shoulder. It was Emma with the fantastic tits that Otto and I both groped with consent. It was late, just after midnight. Our conversation was short and to the point as we decided to leave together. We went back to my place this time to avoid conversations with roommates and wasted boyfriends. We went out on my balcony as we drank and looked up at the stars. "Yup right there, that's the Tiny Dipper," I said, drunk, actually believing my own incorrect constellation names.

"Tiny Dipper? You mean Little Dipper, right?"

"No, it's tiny—that's why it's called tiny. And right there, that's the Big Bopper."

We started making out. We moved inside and fell on the bed, clumsily removing each other's clothes. I went into the bathroom to do whatever it is I did before sex. Tell myself motivational quotes in the mirror. Spray cologne at my groin. You know: guy stuff. When I came back out she was laying on my bed spread-eagled wearing my Green Bay Packers Brett Favre jersey she must have grabbed from my closet. She was wearing that and nothing else. I instantly became hard. Was that gay? Usually I needed physical contact, maybe a bit of hands-on foreplay before I became hard, but the sight of a woman in a man's football jersey made me instantly erect. What was that about? I made a mental note to investigate it further at another time.

The sex was about as good as drunk sex can be. I came, because I was great at sex. Cumming was super easy as always. She faked it because she hadn't quite figured out how to do sex yet. I told her it was okay, she just needed more practice. The next morning, we walked out to my car so I could give her a ride home. At that exact moment my friends showed up in my parking lot to pick up their cars. It was very awkward dialogue, but

I was not ashamed. Emma looked good that morning. They told me Greg got kicked out after we left. He apparently went behind the bar and tried to casually open the cash register. I drove Emma home, kissed her, and told her goodbye. And it was truly a goodbye as I never saw her again. I forgot to get her number. Again. I think I subconsciously felt that I didn't need it. We weren't meant to be. I later found out her cousin was a mutual friend and she told me Emma had moved to Houston, Texas, and got married. I'll never forget the time I made love to a hall of fame quarterback.

23

It's been said time and time again: never shit on your dinner plate… or something along those lines. Don't eat from the toilet. Make sure you separate shitting and eating. Whatever. The message being: never date someone who you cannot avoid on a daily basis. If followed correctly, this rule precludes dating anyone you work with. It is a cogent, rational tenet and one I've failed to obey several times, often in quick succession. When you work in an office with young and ambitious creatives it's almost imperative to have fun inner-office distractions to get you through each tedious week. My favorite inner-office distraction? Flirting. I did not stand alone here. Every office in America hosts several different forms of flirting. It's harmless and makes entering the workplace each day more tolerable, occasionally enjoyable at times. Even married employees have work crushes they flirt with. It's healthy and invigorating and completely normal. They typically mean nothing other than a smidgen of banter and innuendo that alleviates the often uneventfulness of a typical work day.

Sometimes self-control malfunctions or desirability is enhanced, usually both, and that flirting turns into a full-fledged romp-fest. Or maybe just a couple of drunken dates. Regardless of the specifics, it has crossed the theoretical and physical lines of the modern work culture and entered the dangerous point of no return. The unavoidable axis of a failed relationship or hook-up. One of the few enjoyable moments of a failed romance, regardless of how short-lived, is the breath of fresh air you inhale when you realize you don't have to deal with that person or see them ever again. You were probably dreading the awkwardness of the conversation or not-so-subtle hint that you're not interested anymore for at least a week, and when you finally jumped that proverbial last hurdle, there is a wave of relief washing over you and a beautiful sunset of new beginnings beckons. The next one is out there somewhere. You never have to see that person again as far as you know. Well, when you work with that person every single day, that breath of fresh air doesn't happen. You breathe in nitric acid every day, coughing like a dying, pertussis-infected pale-faced child. It's a very uncomfortable phase, a setting that does not pass but is instead now your life.

I knew people that were together, married, happy, etc. who met romantically at their place of work. It could certainly be done and is a very common genesis of a couple's inception. But it's very high-risk/high-reward. I had never been rewarded other than a few cadaverous lays. So far during my time at the firm, I had behaved myself. But that was about to change.

With a new calendar year usually came a few new hires for whatever reason—sackings, suicides, nervous breakdowns, people spontaneously quitting over the festive period. I didn't pretend to know how businesses worked or if it mattered when people were hired, but every January came with additional employees. That New Year we hired two new women. One, Jan, was a coordinator, whatever that meant. No one knew what the coordinator coordinated other than the coffee pot and dishwasher. The other was a very talented graphic designer to work on our ad campaigns named Alanna. I will start by saying I didn't like Jan. At all. She had all the personality of a flat soda. And not even a good type of soda—a flat Diet Shasta Grape. After about two weeks of sitting near her I wanted to push her into a vat of acid each morning. She said things in high-pitched melodic tones as if she was singing. Things like 'Good moooorrrnning!' and whatever else it was that came out of the butthole with teeth that was under her nose. I tried to ignore her when she spoke. She also giggled after everything she said, usually at things that were unequivocally not funny. Cackling and giggling all fucking day. A clucking hen. I was out of the office a lot of the afternoons at meetings or pretending to work from home, but the mornings were my auditory purgatory. I wore headphones. She pierced right through them. I moved into a different part of the office to work from my laptop, her screech traveled the distance between us. It was infuriating. Most women I liked in one way or another, but I strongly loathed Jan. She was annoying. I found her repugnant. Like a cheery, loud snail with hair.

Alanna was the opposite. She was witty and likable. She had good style, somehow making Chuck Taylors look work-appropriate. I was instantly interested in her, but the feeling somewhat diminished when I found out she was taken based on the Claddagh ring on her right-hand ring finger. The traditional Irish band that represents love, and when worn on the right hand with the point of the heart facing the wrist it meant that person is unwed but in a relationship. This did not stop flirting, however. It started very casually. Landing jokes in front of her in group discussions, using her name in conversation, asking about her background. Then we had a project together. We even had a conference call together, just us two locked in the glass room. The eye contact was palpable. Soon after, a co-worker threw one of her periodic Friday night work parties. I rarely went but I made an effort for that one. We developed repartee and birthed inside jokes together. I felt the evolution of a mutual attraction.

Eventually a text was sent. Conversations during the work day sparked and smoldered. This was the sweet spot of any work fling—nothing physical had happened yet but I was excited to go into the office. I wasn't counting too many women on my walk in on those mornings. I wanted to perform my job better each day to impress her. We joked about how punchable Jan was. She rarely mentioned her boyfriend. I shook his hand once at a work outing. It was supple and well manicured. From others I heard he was a putz who was verbally abusive and condescending to her. Scum. Apparently they met in college where she ran cross-country and he played hockey. He was currently on the road playing the semi-pro circuit. He couldn't give up the dream. I don't even think he was getting paid. I mocked him viciously in my head and to my bathroom mirror.

Eventually the texts carried into the weekends and plans were discussed. One fateful Saturday night she was at a bar near my loft. I was out with friends in the Delmar Loop neighborhood but made the trek. I showed up alone and joined her and a few of her friends. There was time for one drink before the bar closed. We chatted and I joked around with her pals, skillfully manipulating them to like me because in that instance it was all that mattered. Friends were everything with most girls. Groupthink was a very real phenomenon. As the lights came on indicating closing time, I proposed my apartment as a destination to the entire group. I referenced my alcohol collection and offered them a place to crash, somehow without sounding too creepy. I could tell Alanna wanted to but looked to her drunk friends for guidance. They looked like they thought just about anything involving the continuance of alcohol was a great idea. I could have proposed an East St. Louis trap house with MD 20/20 and they would have called me a social genius and savior. Eventually we coordinated ourselves and caught an Uber, and made our way back to my place.

Alanna and her friends all grabbed a beer from my fridge and proceeded to have less than three sips before flopping on the couch and air mattress ready for sleep. I cautiously worded an offer to Alanna that she could stay in my bed. She asked if I would join her. I said yes. We spent the night together and talked for a couple hours before passing out. Nothing sexual happened, just an innocuous cuddle. I was the cuddle king. The next morning I drove her friends home and we got breakfast. Two weeks later she broke up with her boyfriend.

24

I had been a part of romantic endeavors with co-workers before in past jobs. Predictably they all ended poorly. The first was at my summer job at RadioShack when I was 18. I had sex with my co-worker Jess and I embarrassingly lasted for just under two minutes. Every time we worked a shift together after that I felt like an inadequate salesperson on the floor. Once I was on the verge of selling a guy our most expensive radio scanner until I looked over at her sneering at my premature closing technique and I botched the sale. Another case was at a marketing internship in college. We texted for a while before making out at a bar. Her breath tasted like what I thought semen would taste like if semen was made from garlic and onions. The next day I was devoid of any romantic interest. I then had to sit five feet from her for the rest of the summer. It was painfully awkward and her constant scowling at me made it worse.

However, with Alanna it felt very different. This was an emotional connection. I genuinely liked her. I was older and wiser and knew the consequences of a failed relationship at work. We became friends first. I treaded lightly and felt sure of my feelings for her. I wanted to resist, but the amorous temptation of a possible long-term partner was too strong and too rare at that point of my life. The more women I dated, the worse my choices were with them. I was learning nothing. Alanna finally felt like a proper fit for me so I decided to ignore my unwritten co-worker rule once again.

We began going on dates. We were 'dating' in the true sense of the verb but not officially together. She met some of my friends, we had sex, she stayed over. Things were progressing nicely... until they weren't. I remember hitting an emblematic wall. Unexpectedly I lost interest for no discernible reason. It was entirely out of the blue. Soon her Chuck Taylors started looking like a silly affectation. Her smile started looking crooked. Her hair was greasy. Her laidback demeanor suddenly seemed vapid and anodyne. She did nothing wrong—nothing changed, but I inexplicably found myself no longer wanting her or even liking her.

I canceled dates. My texts were terse and cryptic. I avoided her desk. Why did this keep happening? Two months ago she seemed like my future wife. I started getting higher totals than normal on my walks to work. Soon any girl that was not her appeared irresistible. I was losing my mind. I loathed this deficiency I had at maintaining relationships. It was discouraging but I knew how I felt and what needed to be done. I had to find a way to break things off, soon. I was truly terrible at this part. I thought about ghosting and gaslighting her in every aspect except work-related undertakings. I realized that probably would not go over well or work long term in any regard. I was a coward. She asked when the next time we could hang out might be. I listed several made-up mundane tasks I had filling up my weekend, like buying a shelf at Menard's, returning the bowling shoes

I accidentally walked out of the local Pin-up Bowl wearing, estate sales, donating plasma and dinner with an old college professor in town on a visit from NYC. She was smart, so it became apparent I had lost a calculable amount of interest and that all these tasks were undeniably made-up... except for Outback Steakhouse with Professor Anstett. That actually happened and was lovely.

Eventually she called me out because I was a weakling afraid of adult conversations or disagreements. I pinned the reasoning on working together and it not being a good idea. She questioned this excuse and asked where the logic was a month ago. I said I was a bit slow at realizing things. She was visibly upset. This conversation happened over text, which in the circumstances I preferred because of said coward status. She reminded me that she broke up with her boyfriend for me. I told her that he's probably still single. She didn't think that was funny or helpful. The conversation eventually came to an end and work became a bitter war of attrition. I requested other designers on projects. I figured things would get better over time. Things never got better. Alanna eventually left the company to move to Cincinnati. I was officially the biggest asshole I knew.

25

St. Louis had always treated a few inches of snow like the second coming of the Black Plague. Now that it was softly falling it was suddenly all anyone could talk about and lives were apparently at risk. The whole city turned into the set of a dystopian post-apocalyptic disaster movie. But that winter's specific snowstorm soon became the worst the city had ever experienced. It was to hit on Friday afternoon and continue all the way to Sunday night; a predicted 6–10 inches of snow over that timespan. The office gave everyone the option to work from home. Everyone except for the bosses knew this was code for a day off.

I had a lunch with a friend just outside downtown and decided to stop at a grocery store before driving home. The shop was in absolute chaos. It looked like the surveillance footage of Black Friday when people enter stores climbing over each other and begin fighting for bargain flat-screen TVs or espresso machines. Except these people were fighting over loaves of bread. I saw two people split a carton of eggs in half because neither would let go, thereby splattering all of them across the floor. It was a war zone. I calmly grabbed a few things to eat for the weekend, not planning to leave the apartment for any reason. I got in line and the wise gentleman in front of me had two 30-racks of beer, a log of Copenhagen chewing tobacco, and he selected a couple of random DVDs off the discount rack while waiting to pay. I guess the guy didn't need any food.

I had gotten home before any real snowfall but turned on the news a while later. It had been severely snowing for a couple hours at this point and the city could not keep up with road maintenance. Every highway was in a complete gridlock, forcing people to abandon their cars to walk or find hotel rooms off the exits. Even a snowplow got stuck. How the fuck does a snowplow get stuck in the *snow*? The one thing it is designed to withstand? That is like a fish drowning or a bird getting vertigo. The news reporters were overjoyed. This was a record-breaking snowstorm. Their chance to really shine as a journalist. Their time to make national news. It was pretty amusing actually. I sat cozily in my apartment for the night, watching movies and then going to bed early like a good boy.

I awoke Saturday to the never-ending snowfall. I lounged for the better part of the day until early evening. I decided this was perfect drinking weather and I poured myself a couple to a few whiskey Cokes. I was not keeping count. After some more drinks I craved human contact, whether that be physically or just verbally. I had no one to shack up with so I decided to venture out on a solo mission. I had a theory that any girl who goes out when it's raining or snowing is what the kids call 'thirsty'. That theory is exponentially multiplied when there is 10 inches of snow on the ground. People need comfort in times of treachery. I was sipping my whiskey, watching football in my apartment, and set on exploring bars by myself until

I received a rather favorable text from my friend Kari.

You in town today? I have a new shorty for you. Shannon and I think you guys would be perfect for each other

Giddy up.

I hopped in a nervous Uber and made way to the 1860 Saloon in Soulard to meet up with my friends Kari, Shannon, and the new shorty. My friend Patrick and his girlfriend lived nearby and enthusiastically joined us, also wanting to get out of the house as well. The shorty's name was Savannah. She was very cute and new to the city. She moved to work for the Purina dog food conglomerate out on Danforth Drive a couple of blocks from the river. Savannah and I ignored the rest of our group with ease and began talking. We were hitting it off. My jokes were going through the uprights from 50-plus yards. She was a sweetheart and had a warmth to her presence. It was like I was talking to a smiley hourglass-shaped space heater with boobs and a human head. We were an hour into the conversation with a first date planned the following week. We seemed highly compatible... until we weren't. Things quickly veered from the simple topic of television shows. She asked for my top five favorites. My five were ingrained into my brain and soul, consistent and irremovable every time the topic of TV came up. It was a monumental top five that I was proud of and had solid reasoning behind it. After I went through my list, her response put me into an uncontrollable fit of rage. She had never watched *Seinfeld*, which I gave a pass to, but she then proceeded to tell me that she had seen *The Office*, but it was not funny and she deemed it stupid.

I am all for opinions, including those that differ entirely to mine, but to say it was 'not funny' and 'stupid' made me want to berate her into the ground, burying her alive under the floorboards beneath her bar stool. I had only had a few drinks at this point, but I recall blacking out while I sermonized violently into her ear for 10 minutes, not letting her an opportunity to retort. I believe I insulted her intellect and personality and possibly her parents several times while praising the show for a barrage of reasons, each better than the last. I unleashed a verbal gunfire of abuse that resulted in her shaking her head and walking away from me and the bar entirely. Kari approached me subsequently and while I was expecting an equally abusive tirade from her, all she whispered was, "I think you're a little too cynical for Savannah. Oh well, let's do a shot."

26

Tuesday morning I was sitting at my desk, trying to turn a deaf ear to Jan's chortling but failing, when my new best friend—co-worker and wingman David—approached me calmly. "Good morning, Chris. How are you today?" Within office walls he had reverted back into his work personality—calm, respectful, and quiet. In a word: dull. I could not tell if this was contrived or subconscious.

"Dave! You sick son of a bitch! What the fuck's going on?!" I said, attempting to prompt Fun David to materialize.

"I have a proposition for you. More of a favor actually."

"I hate favors, Dave." He then began to whisper as he delved into personal matters, "I met a woman recently and this Friday I have four tickets to the Professional Bull Riders' Rodeo. My friend who works in operations at the arena was able to get them for me. I would very much like to take this woman and her friend."

"And you need me to go as well? To occupy this friend?" David nodded yes as I continued. "This friend, how old might she be?"

"Mid-forties I think?" David made a cringey smile

that had a display of 'please, please, please do this'.

"Goddammit. I really wish I had a girlfriend to get me out of things like this. Yeah, Dave, I'll go. But you're paying for the drinks."

Friday arrived and David and I stayed in the office after quitting time to have a beer before meeting Ethel and Bernadette at a nearby wine bar. These were just the names I concocted in my head before meeting them. David said he had to change his clothes. As he walked into the men's bathroom, I couldn't help but notice he did so with a giant duffel bag. Minutes later, out walked a life-sized Sheriff Woody from *Toy Story.* David had noticeably gone overboard on the Wild West gear.

"Jesus Buffalo Bill, who the fuck dressed you?"

"I got all this at Big Bob's Western World off Interstate-55!"

"It looks like you just auditioned for the lead in a *Brokeback Mountain* sequel but didn't get the part because you were *too* gay."

"Ha ha! Good one, pal! I am excited for this!" he said. I don't believe he was familiar with the film.

David was the most suburban-looking-and-acting person I knew. He grew up and remained in the same affluent neighborhood. There was nothing country or rugged about him. He didn't know one end of a cow from the other. This was a blatant appropriation of culture. He emerged from our office virginally sporting a black Stetson's apache buffalo felt fur cowboy hat and a Stetson's plaid flannel western shirt in rust copper tucked into his ridiculous Wrangler cowboy rigid-cut slim-fit jeans. Holding his jeans up was a Montana Silversmith belt buckle encrusted with a silver antlered stag skull that read 'Nice Rack'. He encompassed the $500 outfit with

Tin Haul square-toed cowboy boots with pocket ace playing cards stitched into the sides with the tagline 'Shuffle Dirty'. All his attire was authentic and prohibitively expensive, but with it being all brand new and unworn, from a distance his outfit looked like a children's prepackaged cowboy Halloween costume (holsters sold separately).

We met Thelma and Louise at Bridge Tap House and Wine Bar located in the heart of downtown—a 10-minute walk from the arena. The Bridge was an unpretentious yet high-quality restaurant hidden by scarce signage in the fragmentary block of Tenth and Locust. They had an extensive wine and beer list with shelves of liquor spanning 20 feet on an elegant brick and glossy oak wood bar-back.

The women's names were actually Kristy and Michelle. David was interested in Kristy, but both women were hanging off his every word. His outfit apparently sexually galvanized them. He paired his attire with countless cowboy culture idioms and phrases he must have studied online throughout the day and night before, memorizing them especially for the occasion. David was officially in his element once again.

"The best way to describe a cowboy is mud, blood, guts, and glory, amiright ladies?" David said as the women howled with laughter.

"Oh my goodness, you are just so handsome, David! How on Earth are you single?" asked Kristy's friend Michelle, pumping out musky pheromones.

"Some cowboys have too much tumbleweed in their blood to settle down, little lady. Like me and my guy Christopher here!" I rolled my eyes while letting out a mirthless laugh. The women erupted in laughter once again. Kristy then explained to Michelle diplomatically that David was recently single after a painful divorce.

"Oh, you poor thing David," Michelle said.

"Well, you know what I always say: there's no better place to heal a broken heart than on the back of a horse."

"Jesus Christ," I audibly groaned.

After David generously paid our tab at Bridge, we made our way to Enterprise Arena for the rodeo in a yellow taxi, all funded by David's chivalry. He bought a round of mixed drinks at the ground level liquor cart and we found our seats. He sat in between Kristy and Michelle as he held their attention perpetually with every stupid cowboy quote he uttered, while I was stuck on the other side of Michelle, alone to make comments heard only by myself. I implored Michelle to switch seats with me, emphasizing that we had to sit in our exact designated seat numbers. It sounded like something Greg would say. I was getting noticeably cranky.

As I continued to drink on David's tab, I questioned my ill-temper. Part of me was being crotchety because I felt as though David just dragged me along on this very possible threesome solely to bear witness. But the more I cogitated, the more I unraveled David's greatness as a bachelor. He was God-like, and he held their foaming wide-ons in the palm of his hand. I decided I needed to learn from him. As the rodeo neared its end, David proclaimed his friend in operations was going to get us all down to the dirt to take pictures and meet a couple of the riders. "Giddy up, gals! Come on Christopher!" he said as he exited the row and headed toward the concourse in his new bow-legged gait.

After a couple photos that Kristy, Michelle, and David ever so graciously let me be in, we mingled with a couple of the bull riders and Professional Bull Riders staff. They were contemplating whether to go out to a bar or back to their hotel across the street to party.

"I own a bar!" Kristy verbally ejaculated. "It's closed right now, but I could open it up and we could all go have our own private after-party!" Everyone agreed that was in fact a terrific idea and so we went to Kristy's bar.

27

The bar was located in the Lafayette Square neighborhood. It was just after 11:00 pm when Kristy fumbled her keys out of her purse and into the front door. It was a cozy, exposed-brick Italian café kind of place with a sleek wooden bar to the right upon entry, and two dining room areas to the left. As the cowboy people trickled in, I decided to christen the bar with a new name—Chris's Pub, except with a grave accent, making it Chris's Pubè. I proceeded to slide behind the bar and told Kristy I was the new bartender. Kristy consented, not that it mattered to me. She asked if I wanted to play music from my phone through the stereo via an auxiliary cable. I told Kristy about a recent invention known as Bluetooth. She was not amused. After a half hour of the grand opening of Chris's Pubè, I had over 30 patrons and I was serving them the stiffest drinks in town. They included David, Kristy, Michelle, David's friend from operations, roughly 20 of the PBR rodeo staff, and eight bull riders.

Once I had gifted everyone in the room with a triple-whatever-they-wanted, I decided to augment the party with a hearty dose of Phil Collins. I first played Sussudio—the renowned 1985 No.1 Billboard smash sensation. I felt the aura and air within the room change as the incessant intro drum machine beat powerfully into the eardrums of everyone present. Moods were leisurely lifted to the ceiling as musical delirium erupted throughout Chris's Pubè. I was the best DJ in St. Louis. As the song was closing, I began looking through Phil's back catalog. I quickly came to the terminal realization that nothing could top the legendary hit song, so I played Sussudio again. And again. I played Sussudio seven times before one of the bull riders, a brute called Bubba, motioned me over. I greeted him cheerfully only to have him tell me through clenched teeth that if I played Sussudio one more time he was going to jump over the bar and beat the shit out of me. I smoothly segued away from Phil Collins.

As the night wore on, David's exploits became noticeable to the entire room. He jumped on top of the bar to the song Hungry Like the Wolf by Duran Duran and began howling. He then grabbed a random bottle and started pouring liquor into people's mouths from above. Kristy and Michelle yelled for David, and as he looked over, they simultaneously flashed him to a round of cheers from everyone. He danced along the bar top and screamed, "THIS IS MY ELEMENT!"

The remainder of the evening-slash-early morning was hazy, but I recalled seeing David make out with both women at certain points and had one of the bull riders straddling his back as he crawled around the floor on his hands and knees making horse noises. The party eventually came to a reluctant end as people retired one by one for the night. I too decided it was time to go home. My phone was dead from playing Sussudio on a loop. As I walked out from behind the bar, I found David passed out in a booth with one arm around Kristy and the other draped around Michelle. It was 6:00 am. I walked home in the brisk winter air as the sun came up, the emerging colors of dawn transforming the city sky.

28

To reiterate, in my several years as a single miscreant I had an on-again, off-again relationship with dating apps. As mentioned I preferred to meet women in person but eventually I got bored or lonely or desperate and in a pursuit of companionship I would download, delete, and redownload ad infinitum.

Most of it turned out to be a massive waste of time, exchanging meaningless messages never to meet or liking hundreds of profiles never to be matched. It was a fun window shopping activity to keep me occupied while passing bowel movements, but it never gained many results. There was however the occasional first date. I'd say dating apps garnered one a month on average for me over the years when I used them. They usually went well. This particular first date did *not* go well, at least from my perspective. She had a great time. I will explain.

Her name was Emily. Cute blonde, relatively fit with a nice smile and had what appeared to be a good personality based on the short conversation we had. I started the chitchat with a subtle yet direct, "Butt stuff?"

She realized I was clearly joking (for the most part) and responded with, "Recipient or donor?" We began talking and arranged to meet at a bar in the Central West

End. I had no qualms about the meeting. I was very optimistic. I drank a beer in my car on the way over to loosen up and arrived a few minutes early. I ordered another beer at the bar and waited patiently, eyeing the entrance every 15–20 seconds or so.

At last, 13 minutes late a girl who looked like Emily but much heavier and ragged entered the bar. Her face looked like she probably had bad breath. She was coming towards me. I thought maybe she sent her older, tired, worn-out sister in first to get a glimpse of me—a recce, if you will. Then she smiled and greeted me, opening her arms wide for a hug.

Oh God. This was Emily. A bloated, inflated version of the photos I had been looking at over the last few days. I had gotten swindled by some pathetic catfishing predator who used to look pretty but now doesn't.

When many people think of getting catfished, they have visions of 55-year-old overweight men with pizza sauce-stained sweatpants in their mom's dark, computer-lit basement posing as a 23-year-old Victoria's Secret model. But that is simply the exaggerated extreme. A catfish by definition is any fabrication or misrepresentation of a person's dating profile in relation to their actual self. It could be lying about their profession, college degree, age, or in this case using very, very old photos of a much more desirable past self. So *by definition*, Emily was a catfishing predator.

I was not a shallow person or a verbal body-shamer, never have been. I always understood the importance of personality and the inner-being, et cetera. But attraction is imperative in a relationship and an equally important component of a companion. I was not attracted to the present-day Emily who slumped on the bar stool beside me. I had a whirlwind of emotions going on at that moment. Embarrassment, anger, confusion, disappointment, and a small trace of lust. To her credit, her boobs were substantially bigger thanks to the surplus weight.

I had a dilemma to wrestle with. Well not really, I knew I was stuck for a few drinks at least—I'm not a monster. But in reality, I think in that position I should have been able to walk out at that very moment without any remorse or guilt about Emily's feelings. She was the one being dishonest. I was the victim—I had been deceived, mis-sold, defrauded, fucking led up the garden path. I had gone out with girls who were not conventionally fit in the past. Did that make me a hero? No, of course not, but if people were to call me one I would humbly accept the accolade.

But while her disproportionate figure was certainly one reason for my displeasure, it was more so that I had been sold burnt matches. Sure, the photos were her but a version of her before she became a burnt-out exercise exile. She knew what she was doing. How could she ever expect to start an honest relationship on that foundation?

I was three sips into my first drink and already plotting my exit. But I couldn't just walk out. That would be mean. I was never mean to women, only the voices in my head were and I tried hard not to listen to them. So I started to brainstorm ideas on how to get out of there. I did this while giving her eye contact and nodding, pretending to listen while she spoke about her job or cats or family or whatever else it was she was boring on about.

As I've mentioned before, modern day romantic comedies have ruined the fake phone call move. I tried to be more strategic. I contemplated spilling my entire beer on my plain white T-shirt so I could have an excuse to go home. I thought about starting a small fire in the bathroom trash can so we had to evacuate the bar. I daydreamed about telling her the whole thing was too soon and make up an ex-girlfriend who tragically died in a planking incident last month. All these ideas were incredibly stupid and very implausible. I decided to go with ol' reliable and drink until I began enjoying myself. I knew I wouldn't see her again, so her judgment of my intake didn't really bother me. I asked if she wanted a shot. She said yes. We did a shot. I chugged the rest of my beer in an excuse for a chaser. I then ordered a 12.6% alcohol beer next, something I rarely did.

We continued to drink and converse, and not only was she unappealing visually, but she was actually a terrible person. She started talking about her family issues and how in an altercation with her sister she had to, "beat that bitch down." She said this with blood-curdling articulation and a wagging finger. We ended up going to another bar. This would have been a perfect time to leave and excuse myself as I needed to get home to let out the imaginary dog or feed the non-existent cat, but I was in the middle of a perfect drinking buzz and it was impossible to stop immediate intake in that moment.

So we walked down the street to an Irish pub and ordered another couple of drinks. At this point she was convinced that I actually liked her. I had chosen the wrong profession. I was a magnificent actor. A consummate liar. A suave con-artist that only used his skills to avoid hurting someone's feelings even though they absolutely deserved it.

As she babbled on and on, I again pretended to listen intently while thinking about how I would end the date.

Casual hug? Firm double-pump handshake? Should I dap her up? Surely not a kiss or suggest a nightcap? We finished our drinks and I said I had to get going for whatever reason. As we started walking out, she kept pace with me and it suddenly occurred to me: my tactical first-date strategy of choosing a place near her home had backfired. She took an Uber to the bar. As I was sticking with the whole 'be a good person' script I knew I had to give her a ride home. I was very upset with myself now, as well as with her. We got into my car and I played music just loud enough to ensure a lack of conversation. It was only about an eight-minute drive. Two songs. As we pulled up to her place she said, "We should definitely do this again." For some inexplicable reason I responded with, "Yeah, we totally should." What a fucking idiot.

It was just after I uttered those words that she moved in to kiss me. I couldn't help respect the forwardness and urgency displayed with the move. As her lips hit mine I for some reason became aroused and we started making out pretty aggressively. Hands were being thrown into intimate areas and guttural noises were made. At that point if she would have asked me to come in I probably would have. Luckily, she instead just gave me a goofy smile and got out the car and said we'd talk soon.

No we won't, I thought to myself. The next morning she texted me, trying to execute an inside joke she thought we already had going on based on our conversation the night before. I never responded. It was the first person I can recall properly 'ghosting'. I usually just displayed less and less interest in my texts or prolonged hanging out until the girl got the message or became too frustrated. I was the worst kind of guy in that regard. Just ask Alanna. I think most girls would rather be told it's over or even be ghosted so they knew within a couple days which way the wind was blowing. I usually wasted their time for weeks dancing around like a gutless mouse. But I wanted nothing to do with this girl in the slightest. I was still bothered by her, hey-check-out-these-photos-from-seven-years-ago-where-I-was-working-out-three-times-a-week-and-had-great-metabolism-but-now-I-look-like-Snorlax-with-bad-makeup-but-you'll-never-know-until-you-meet-me-and-I'll-just-rely-on-my-abhorrent-personality-to-get-you-to-love-me strategy.

Classic.

29

The very next day I deleted Tinder. Not entirely because of Machiavellian Emily but she was certainly the stout straw that broke this thirsty camel's back. Poor camel. In times like this, whether it be a failed first date or a finished fling, I often felt a contradicting combination of hopefulness and loneliness. Sometimes in those instances with no female prospects on the horizon, I would think back to women from my past that I could have been wrong about or never gave a fair chance. Where were they now? I would type in the St. Louis area codes '314' and '636' into my contact list and peruse all the women I had an interest in at one point or another. This was only a palliative. It was a short-term solution to a long-term problem of mine, but I did it time and time again.

I found myself exercising this tactic again the next day, and halfway through scrolling I came across Mandi. The pretty girl who hit my car. It was a hazy evening the night I met her and brought her back to my apartment after a lot of drinks, only to pass out in front of her with a limp cocaine dick. We exchanged a few meager texts shortly after but not enough to amount to a second encounter. I am not sure what I found so wrong in her that dismissed the thought of another meeting. So I texted her. It was always awkward contacting someone you ceased conversation with. All the flow and momentum, or however little of it there was, had a very short half-life. I used to think of myself as a bit of an oracle of texting eloquence, but had certainly had my fair share of mishaps, much like the 'welp' fiasco.

Heyyy

Simple yet crafty and cunning. The extra 'y's implied romantic interest and suggested something vaguely sexual. Guys have been using 'Heyyy' since the mid-seventies when Arthur Fonzarelli made his way to living room television sets across America. It left it to the recipient's imagination. As long as it was not sent after 9:00 pm, it usually elicited some sort of a response. Maybe a 'ha ha what's up?' or a 'fuck off Chris', but anything was better than silence.

Mandi responded with glee and naïveté like the poor driver she was, and we started talking again—only this time with intent and purpose. We met a week later for drinks and a late-night pizza. It was fun and casual. The night was ended with an ardent makeout and plans to see each other again. We both had the upcoming weekend available and decided to play it by ear.

That Thursday I received one of the most random, intriguing, and disturbing texts I'd ever received to date. It was from my friend Bob. In a word, Bob was afuckinganimal. He was a lumberjack of a man whose insides were forged in a melting pot of drugs and alcohol. Always the life and soul of the party. And then the death of it. Followed by the resurrection of it. Bob was one of the most fun people I'd ever known in my life. He was Dan Bilzerian without the money and tits and assault rifles and legion of Instagram fans.

Bob usually came and went in my life. We'd spend a

couple weekends going out together and then I wouldn't hear from him for months on end. We were currently in a trough in this cycle, so the text was an enticing surprise. It read: *Want to come to a sex party Saturday night? You just have to bring a chick.*

No 'hello'. No 'hey man how've you been?' Just a 'want to come to a sex party in two days?' Not necessarily out of character but it was certainly a first.

I was initially hesitant until I quickly wised up and concluded, of course I want to go to a sex party. But deciding if I wanted to go or not was far from the problem. Finding a willing female participant was. It felt near impossible. Who the fuck would want to go to a sex party with me? I then thought of Mandi, as she was the closest thing to a sexual partner I had at that moment, despite the fact we hadn't had sex yet. I realized that if I asked her to come, whether she agreed or declined there was no chance of ever dating this girl. I could not date a chick who had been to a sex party, could I? She could not possibly want to date me, could she? Might as well have Pornhub as my homepage. I told Bob I would go if I could find a girl. He responded like he was Liam Neeson in a worldwide box office action-thriller: *You have 2 hours*

Apparently planning a sex party was somewhat complicated. It was not just an event where invites are sent out and people who can make it show up. It was very meticulous. At least this one was. There was a guest list put together using a fine-tooth comb, an exacting screening process, and a target number of participants, including an equal number of corresponding genders. A couple had apparently dropped out, prompting Bob's text to me of all people.

In all honesty I highly doubted Mandi would want to

go. In even more honesty, I was fully prepared for her to call me a pig and exclaim she would never talk to me again. If I remembered correctly, she told me she didn't do drugs the night we met. She was obviously a pompous prude, disgusted by the idea of a sex party, or so I thought. But I really wanted to go and would have felt guilty inviting anyone else first. So I threw a Hail Mary. And then I recited one of them.

My text was rendered as fluently as possible to sound persuasive yet nonchalant. The possibility of the sex party relied solely on how I worded that text. I wanted to preface with a somewhat apologetic explanation that this was not a normal occurrence, but I wanted it to sound fun and spontaneous while uninhibited. It's just a sex party after all, no big deal! Live a little! When I felt I had the perfect sculpture of words, I hit send.

This is really weird but do you want to go to a sex party with me? I've never been

Her response was equally as eloquent.
Sure

30

After sending in 'headshots' and signing a disclaimer we were officially on the guest list for Saturday night. On the exclusive invite they had designated a 60-minute 'cocktail hour' like it was a fucking wedding reception. Aside from that I had no idea what to expect, other than the obvious. Bob told me to dress nice. That was somewhat ludicrous to me. It was a sex party. Why in the hell would your clothes matter? I asked Bob this; he was not amused. He took his sex parties very seriously.

Mandi and I arrived promptly on time because we were very nervous and didn't want to upset the sex party people. We shared an apprehension like we were meeting the mafia. Mandi looked great. She wore a tight short red cocktail dress with her hair down and alluring bright cherry lipstick. I envisioned what type of underwear she chose for the occasion. I feel like a sex party is the type of event that would inspire a girl to go shopping for lingerie. I knew nothing about women. I wore a slim-fit black blazer over a black T-shirt, dark blue jeans, and nice dress boots. Upon arrival I realized I was somewhat underdressed. All the other guys were wearing full suits, some with ties. Imagine wearing a three-piece suit and a tie to an event where the primary basis was to be naked the entire time. I figured I would try to be naked first and get all the girls while the other guys struggled to find tie racks and wooden hangers for their pleated dress slacks. Idiots.

Bob was late so Mandi and I stood in the entryway aimlessly for a few minutes until we were greeted by the host, a man who went by the name of 'Lizard Dick'. I made a mental note to take a quick but investigative glance at his member during the festivities later to see how he earned the nickname. Lizard Dick could not have been more gracious. "So how do you two know each other?" he asked.

"She crashed into my car," I said.

He told us to relax, that it was completely normal to be nervous the first time. He offered us wine and various drugs. Mandi stuck to white wine while I took a fair-sized dab of MDMA, 100 mg of Viagra, and a lovely glass of Cabernet Franc. Before the MDMA hit I took a moment to digest Mandi's contrasting morals. Drugs were apparently not okay, but sex parties are done without contemplative thought. What an interesting creature I had on my arm.

We began mingling with other couples. I couldn't help but notice guys ogling Mandi head to toe like they were picking out a cut of veal from the supermarket. I didn't understand the rules of a sex party. Was Mandi fair game to all these guys? I had not even had sex with her yet. Would I have to watch her get passed around like a ceremonial pipe? I was overthinking things. As the MDMA kicked in I began to relax and enjoy myself.

Bob arrived halfway through the cocktail hour. As he entered the room, people reacted like Heath Ledger had just fallen naked from the sky, resurrected and tumescent for the sole benefit of this fuck fest. Hugs, handshakes, and ass grabs made way to Bob and his beautiful date Crystal. He was a living legend to these sex party people. Where did Bob meet them? I made a mental note to ask him another time.

We continued to mingle and exchange pleasantries and niceties for another half an hour until I noticed two couples duck into the master suite of the three-bedroom apartment. Subsequently, my new friend Lizard Dick came over and pleasantly informed us that some of the couples were getting started, but not to start until we felt we were ready. Lizard Dick should author a book on hosting parties, I thought to myself.

I was nowhere near ready, but I severely doubted that I would ever be so I conferred with Mandi and we decided to have one more drink and then make our way into the bedroom. Bob and Crystal agreed that this was logical. I chose a double vodka club and downed it quickly.

As we made our way into the bedroom of a thousand fucks, I was half-horny and half-nervous. This was no different to most of my sexual encounters to date, but in this instance it was heightened by strangers and psychoactive drugs.

As we crossed the threshold of the bedroom door, we saw a couple sitting on the windowsill and making out, still clothed. As we walked in further we saw the king-sized bed, comfortable chairs, and chaise lounges. If someone ignorant of sex party etiquette walked into this bedroom, they would have thought, wow what an elegant and beautiful boudoir with a king-sized bed and handsome chaise lounges and large comfy chairs! Look at all the pillows! I love the candy apple red silk sheets and luxurious soft furnishings. And no TV! What dignified and tasteful people must live here. I bet they read and have enlightening conversations every night before bed as they go to sleep and dream about grand adventures and exotic experiences. *Wrong.* As someone walking in for the first time but still somewhat aware of what happens at sex parties, I thought with ultimate conviction that the bedroom was elaborately set up for gang banging. I made my third mental note of the night to ask Lizard Dick if he designed the bedroom himself or if there were dark-web sex party interior decorators one could hire.

There was a man sitting on the bed with a woman on each side playfully touching each other and necking. As I walked in nervously holding Mandi's hand, he looked up at me and smirked, giving me a slight head nod like I was some rich asshole whose car he had just valeted and taken for a joy ride without my knowledge, returning it without a scratch but an interior full of valet farts. I didn't want to upset this sex party veteran, fearful of him inserting himself into Mandi with a snap of his fingers, so I gave a fearful grin back with an awkward robotic head nod.

I looked over to Bob for guidance. He didn't offer any as he had pinned Crystal up against the wall whispering sweet nothings in her ear. Mandi and I moved over to an extra wide chaise lounge chair in the corner. My entire body was now overcome with a sense of warmth from the MDMA hit. Looking back, I believe it was just another effect of the methamphetamine, but at that moment I was certain I was sitting in the comfiest chair I had ever experienced in my entire life. I started rubbing the arms' fabric with a sense of euphoria. Mandi and I figured we should just get started and pretend no one else was around. This worked. Or possibly it was just the Viagra I took an hour ago. Regardless we both became very aroused from kissing and touching and began taking off our clothes.

Mandi then got on top of me. It was happening! It was in! I was sex partying! I announced this to the entire room to a reception of cheers. I noticed the centerpiece bed was now filled with several more naked or undergarment-wearing bodies. It looked like a giant game of Twister... if adults were playing and you had to be naked with an erection. We continued for a while and decided while we now had sex party experience, we were still novices and stuck to our chaise lounge corner. The one thing I was confused about was cumming. How long was this party supposed to go on for? It did not specify on the invitation. Do I cum right before I plan to leave or do the guys cum multiple times? I wanted to ask Lizard Dick, but he seemed pretty busy.

Mandi and I eventually decided to move over to the extra-large padded bench at the end of the bed and get closer to the action. As we did this, a gentleman approached both of us in a most pleasant fashion and said to me, "Sorry mate, but do you mind if I have sex with your beautiful partner," and motioned to Mandi, "that is if you are interested?" Before I could answer, Mandi responded, "Oh, thank you! But I am going to keep having sex with him for now."

"Of course," said the gentleman with a genuine smile. "Enjoy each other."

"Jesus, what is this place?" I whispered to Mandi. "I feel like we're in Charles Manson's cult."

Mandi and I began having sex on the bench. I did not

want to be the first guy to cum and I also wasn't sure where to do it. Everything in the room was so nice. It sounded like the girls were allowed to cum whenever they wanted. I heard a lot of female orgasms. I don't think Mandi knew she could cum, though. It was her first sex party after all.

About 10 seconds later I came. Mandi and I put on our underwear and went back into the living room and made ourselves another drink. We stayed and talked for one, refilled and went back into the bedroom revitalized and ready for more sex party. On my earlier entrance into the bedroom I felt like a wounded sheep, helplessly wandering through a field in search of my separated mother. So fragile and frightened. On my second entrance, I felt like a widely loved professional wrestler making my way down the entrance ramp to the ring with the accompaniment of my theme music, strobes, and a smoke machine with cheers of adoring fans in a sold-out arena. I was a God among mere mortals. Mandi grabbed me as we entered and asked, "Do you want me to find another girl for us?" I responded carefully.

"Do you?"

"Yeah, kinda? I don't want to sleep with any other guys, but another girl would be fun."

"Whatever you want is fine by me Mandi."

She hadn't even found another girl yet and I was already more than half hard at the idea. She searched the room until she noticed an uneven number of women on the bed and guided me towards the right side of the mattress. The second girl she asked was named Jess, and she obliged and became our third partner. I made my final mental note to later ask Mandi what the exact response was from the first girl who declined.

They each straddled one of my legs and began kissing my body while intermittently making out with one another, with Jess grabbing my member zealously. Eventually our new friend began performing oral sex on me as I did the same to Mandi. It was naked poetry. We did this for a while until I threw a dong bag on and started having sex with Jess. I made sure to keep this somewhat short-lived to be respectful of Mandi. I'm such a considerate guy, I thought to myself as I mounted this complete stranger I met 10 minutes ago. After half an hour composed of watching, engaging, watching, masturbating, watching, and engaging, I finally finished with Mandi. We both agreed at this point we did enough to fully experience the sex party. We put our clothes back on and hung out in the living room. We invited Jess but she chose to wait in line to have sex with Lizard Dick in the shower.

Bob and Crystal came out and joined us as we drank and laughed about the absurdity of sex parties. It was a very weird but great night.

31

While Mandi certainly displayed several attributes of an admirable life counterpart by participating in a sex party with me—very successfully I might add—I think we both knew there was no future in it. There were a few texts sent to one another after that night. Like, *hey remember when we went to a sex party at a guy named Lizard Dick's apartment? That was pretty weird LOL.* But we never actually saw each other again after that night. I certainly found a lot about that fact disconcerting and mystifying but I chose not to over think it. That is the fickle thing about love; one night you're having sex with each other in front of 20 strangers, and the next you've both withered away into nothingness. I chose not to tell anyone about the sex party. Not because it was embarrassing to me, but more because it felt braggy. I didn't want to intimidate people with my extracurricular activities of upscale orgies on MDMA. Too boastful for my liking.

The following Monday at work I was still very much hungover from the drugs and alcohol served to me on 14-inch round and chrome-plated serving trays the Saturday night before. At this point I was a regular Monday morning Adderall customer of my neighbor Christina. I took one just before our weekly meeting to be livelier. I also had a pitch idea for a local church later in the day that I still needed to complete... or actually start. The meeting was trivial as usual, except for Greg's accomplishment.

"Greg, win for last week?" our boss asked.

"I moved into my new apartment." Greg said this as if he was going from one place to another, not from his parents' house as a 33-year-old man-child.

"Oh, great! What area?"

"Soulard."

A historic neighborhood in the city, Soulard was mostly known for its raucous bars and nice restaurants, many being known for live jazz and blues. Soulard was arguably the most frequented drinking neighborhood in all of St. Louis, especially by those in their early twenties. While I loved the neighborhood and hung out there often, I found it an interesting choice for Greg to move to at 33. However, it was close to work and a long way from his childhood bedroom, so I supported his decision.

Back at our desks, I queried the decision. "What prompted the move Greg?"

"Had enough of my mom. Time to be free, flap my wings."

"I think you could argue that time was 13 years ago."

"Fuck you."

"So why Soulard?"

"Why not?" he said with contempt. "It's what the kids are doing."

"Speaking of that, do you have a room for Joseph there? You know, your son?"

"No."

"So where the hell is he going to sleep when he's with you?"

"I'm buying a couch, Christopher."

"Father of the year award right here."

He asked if I wanted to come by Friday after work to have some drinks and check out his new living quarters. Easy yes. I was dying to see this charming rat hole he'd gotten himself. Work was always easier with something at the end of the week to look forward to.

I dedicated the rest of the day to the local Catholic church project. In their inquiry they expressed a concern over the lack of young adults at their services. They hired our firm to help create a commercial that would incite more young people to attend mass. I was not quite sure why my boss decided to delegate this project to me, an atheist border-line alcoholic and drug abuser, but I accepted the challenge. I tried to conjure up reasons that would make a Catholic church service appealing to millennial jack-offs. I really struggled to find any thing other than the free wine, so as per usual I decided to use comedy as a way of swindling dumb idiots watching TV to do something they probably didn't want to do.

With the recent departure of the St. Louis Rams NFL organization, people were hurting. I decided to use this sorrow against them in an attempt to brainwash them into having something to do on Sundays. Mental conditioning. In my opinion the best part of going to pro football games was always the tailgating. As this idea came into my brain, I immediately decided I was ready for the meeting. I worked better with improvisation. When I had presentations or speeches prepared, I was too nervous. I had a general idea; I would unleash the rest at the meeting the next morning.

The next day I arrived at St. Anthony's Catholic Church, triple espresso induced and wearing a one-size-fits-most beer drinking helmet and a foam finger that had 'God #1' written on it in sharpie. I wasted no time getting into my commercial pitch.

"All right, as a somewhat young person myself I can tell you this: to get the youth through your door you have to make church seem as a fun and sociable event where they would be *seen*. That's what young people want. To be seen by their peers. They want a party. So we have to make church *seem* like a party. And how do you party on a Sunday? By tailgating. Sunday mass. Gameday in the Catholic community. The holy spiritual gridiron. The Rams are gone, football in St. Louis is no more. This is your chance to take advantage of people's empty Sundays. I want to make a commercial featuring people tailgating in the church parking lot on a Sunday morning, excited for Father Ned's beautiful 9:00 am service. We can have people in #1 football jerseys with 'God' on the back and oversized foam fingers. They will be tossing the football, playing bags, and grilling hamburgers with Christian hymns playing throughout. We could have a ticket scalper offering up front-row pew seats, free of charge of course, and young people embracing each other with high-fives and hugs in honor of God's grace. We finish the commercial with everyone getting in line to squeeze through your doors and display a 360 aerial shot of your beautiful church's interior with a list of all your services. Thoughts?"

The St. Anthony's front office bristled with excitement and Father Ned cracked a smile as they asked me when we could get to work. This job is a fucking joke, I thought to myself.

Friday arrived and I was so excited I didn't even need my newly administered daily helping of amphetamine.

On the walk to work that morning I saw eight women I found sexually attractive. I usually snuck out of the office early Friday afternoons or left at lunch, but with Greg being a stickler for 'the rules' I impatiently waited with him until 5:00 pm. Not 4:56, not 5:03: 5:00 pm CST. I got into the front seat of his Nissan Altima in the parking ramp, shuffling Gatorade bottles, Chick-fil-A wrappers, and Walgreens white prescription bags out of the way on the passenger side floorboard with my feet. He had the same Nickelback Dark Horse album in his CD player. I was convinced it was stuck. He said he just really liked it.

After a brief drive into the heart of Soulard we arrived at his brick duplex. The only entrance was through a fence door into a courtyard that he called his front yard. I couldn't help but notice as Greg entered his apartment that he didn't use a key. I inquired about this. "You don't keep your door locked?"

"It's broken. Some idiot kicked it in last weekend."

"Who are you hanging out with? Why are people breaking into your apartment?"

"None of your concern, Christopher." He always called me Christopher despite the several attempts of mine to insist it was just Chris. "Apparently the guy is coming by in a bit with some help to fix it for me."

"Oh, great."

The apartment itself was appallingly small. It was essentially two rooms and a bathroom. With just one foot inside, we were standing in the front door, the entryway, the living room, and the kitchen all at the same time like it was the Four Corners Monument of Utah, Colorado, Arizona and New Mexico. The left side of the wall consisted of a counter with basic kitchen appliances and a few shelves mounted above. There was a small strip of kitchenette tiling to insinuate the official 'kitchen', while the rest of the room was carpeted. He had no pantry so alongside the counter was a mobile wire shelf with boxes of Uncle Ben's brown rice, Fruity Pebbles, and shrimp ramen packets. *Shrimp.* What a fucking weirdo. I took a mental inventory of Greg's belongings in the living room. It was fascinating. He had a 55-inch flat screen TV sitting on the floor leaning against the wall with no stand and about 10 DVDs. Of those DVDs, three were seasons of *Seinfeld*, five were various *Fast and the Furious* movies, and rounding out the collection were two exact copies of *The Big Lebowski*. He had a desk sitting in the middle of the room, where he said the couch would eventually go, and on it I couldn't help but notice a heap of bills. As he used the bathroom, I took a closer look. I picked up his credit card statement for the last month. Some of the establishments listed included the Harley Davidson gift shop, Toys R' Us, Quesadilla Town (three times), TJ Maxx, US Post Office, Taco Bell twice in a row, and Quesadilla World. It consisted mostly of fast food restaurants, some of which I didn't think people actually ate at, such as Quesadilla Town, and the bill somehow amounted to close to $500. He said that while living at his parents' house he would never eat dinner with them, always procuring his own meals. Such an interesting life form, it was good he now had a Petri dish to call his own.

I asked to use his bathroom despite not having to go. I had to see his medicine cabinet. I carefully closed the door behind me. Of course there was no lock. He had one yellow towel crumpled on the floor, no shower curtain and an empty toilet paper holder. I quickly opened the mirror door to what appeared to be a flourishing pharmaceutical catalog. It was a magnificent assemblage of pharmaceuticals. Prozac, Cymbalta, Hydroxyzine, Ambien, Niravam, Abilify, Bupropion Hcl, and an abundance of different hair restorative drugs. I opened a drawer below to also find a NutraStim professional hair growth laser comb, FDA-approved and clinically tested. I thought to myself, if even half of these drugs are priced at out-of-pocket along with this ostensibly expensive laser comb, it's no question why he has lived at home for the last decade. There were thousands of dollars' worth of pills in front of me, some obviously expired. I put everything back as it was and flushed the toilet for effect. Exiting the bathroom, I caught a glimpse of Greg's bedroom. It was a bare mattress with no box spring laid in the center of the room with clothes everywhere. "Greg, how the hell is your room this messy already?"

"My suitcase exploded."

32

Another interesting factoid about Greg was that he rarely drank at this time in his life. He proclaimed it gave him rhabdomyolysis the next day if he indulged too much. Greg was notorious in his parents' neighborhood urgent care center for repeatedly admitting himself for routine hangovers, maintaining that it was his death knell.

But on this Friday night he explained to me that this was new Soulard Greg and he found a medication that alleviated his rhabdo symptoms after drinking. He then started calling himself Party Greg. "Party Greg is out tonight!" he randomly yelled. He had a bottle of Captain Morgan and a two liter of Coca-Cola. He proceeded to go on a rant about how regular Coke was better than Diet Coke because of aspartame and less bloating. I hadn't had a drink yet, so I just quietly agreed with him. When Greg was adamant about things, regardless of how obscure or random, he usually did his research. I could tell he was waiting for me to be the contrarian so he could aggressively reference facts, statistics, and studies. I did not give him the pleasure.

After another couple drinks waiting for his friends to fix his door, Greg turned our conversation to his interest in porn. Didn't even segue it, just began talking about porn. "The other day I was watching deleted scenes and a director's interview from a porno and you would not believe what goes on on set."

"What the hell made you want to watch deleted porn scenes?"

"It was more for the director's cut. It was fascinating. Do you know what a fluffer is?"

"No."

"It's the person on set who keeps the male actor hard in between shots. I think that is pretty honest work if you can get it. If I was gay I would consider it. Really not that difficult. Just need to keep the stimulation nice and steady. And you don't have to be on camera or have your name in the credits but you earn a nice little paycheck."

"So you're telling me your dream job is to be a fluffer?"

"No, I'm saying it's a decent job."

"Better than advertising?"

"Certainly not worse."

"I can't agree with you. What else did you learn?"

"At any second of the day there are as much as 30 million unique visitors viewing porn. This means that there are about 30 million people viewing porn right now. And now. And now... and now. Also, did you know that the most searched porn-related word in America is 'creampie'? Pornhub did an in-depth analysis. 'Teen' is also very popular."

"Very enlightening."

Greg continued talking about porn, switching to his own fixations. "Also, lately I haven't been able to get off unless the guy is black."

"How in the fuck would that help you get off?"

"I don't know. It is just better for me when he's black.

It's a bit weird."

"But you're white. Don't you want to envision yourself in the scenario?"

"Fuck no. I would never screw those girls. They're in porn."

"I don't think you understand how porn works."

"I know more than most. I watch the director's cuts."

"Are the girls black?"

"No, they're white."

"Again, I think a therapist might be able to help you. Maybe."

"Saw one once. Helped him fix his computer."

"Yeah I know, you told me."

Suddenly, the door flew open at a crooked angle as one of the hinges was off. The loose frame jiggled like a door stop spring. "Don't do that!" Greg yelled as his friend Brian busted into the apartment.

"Hey gentleman!" Brian said and shook my hand while introducing himself. Following Brian was his friend Jeremy carrying a tool box. Greg looked at Jeremy and asked, "Are you the help?"

"Sure am."

"Jesus."

Against all of Greg's odds, they fixed the door. They found the task rather easy and mocked Greg relentlessly for needing two men to come over and fix a simple door hinge and frame. I liked Brian and Jeremy. They stayed and drank with us. They had known Greg for close to a decade and this was evident in the way they spoke to him. They belittled him with slights and insults that Greg did not enjoy. But unlike the spiky version of him I've seen in the office, he took it like a puppy rolling over on its back for a belly rub. He seemed helpless. It was fantastic.

I really liked Brian and Jeremy. We had a couple more drinks and headed to a new warehouse bar called The Cockpit. It might have been the douchiest bar I had ever encountered but it was stuffed with sexual delicacies. Dozens and dozens of girls in short, clingy, flimsy outfits on despite the winter weather. There were an equal number of contemptible male counterparts, all sporting the same European frat haircut and Ralph Polo button-ups with personalities just as anodyne as their outfits, but it was still the place to go on the weekend to meet women. Riverfront Times named it 'St. Louis' Best Bar to Get Laid At'. Greg said he wanted to find a thirsty power hoosier, whatever that meant.

As we got to the entrance, we were abruptly stopped by the bouncer and informed that Greg was not allowed in. I immediately laughed but then inquired as to why not. "He's wearing wind pants," the bouncer responded in monotone.

"They are Reeboks. They cost me $45," Greg said in contempt.

"Sorry, bud. Pretty strict dress code policy tonight. It's the only thing they are sticklers for in this place."

"I plan on buying several drinks."

"Yeah, that's how bars usually work. Sorry man. Go home and change and I'll let you cut the line when you get back."

"Crock of shit!"

"But you three are good to go in. No cover yet."

We all looked at Greg for a moment, contemplating the move. Greg scorned us not to go in without him and that we try a different bar.

"Sorry dude, I don't want to be seen with someone wearing wind pants. Embarrassing!" Jeremy said with a smirk. I felt a bit of allegiance to Greg at the time for the sole fact he invited me out and I just met his friends. I told him I would go to another bar with him, but he changed his mind and pleaded for me to go in and not to let him ruin my night. So dramatic. He got in a cab and went home as I went into the bar with Jeremy and Brian, my loyalty unscathed to my work friend.

The bar turned out to be very uneventful. We took shots and mocked people satirically without their acknowledgement and got loser drunk. We spoke few complete sentences to women. Brian and Jeremy went home to their respective girlfriends. I took an Uber to my apartment and ate pizza before falling asleep while trying to jerk off. It was a sad commentary on the average guy's Friday night in St. Louis.

33

The following Monday on my way to work I saw zero women I wanted to sleep with. I didn't look up from the sidewalk. Greg's 'win' was getting his door frame fixed. I did very little work that day. I found myself in an odd state of melancholy. I think it derived from Saturday night and, perhaps more holistically, my dating woes at the time and the stark realization that I would be alone for the rest of my life. While being endlessly single certainly had its perks, the cons seemed to outweigh the pros. I went down a Google rabbit hole of the effects of loneliness. One article said seclusion was a strong predictor of premature death, terrible mental health, and lower quality of life. This article sank my mood into an even lower state of darkness. It talked about loneliness being an actual health problem that doctors should be looking at. It compared a poor social and emotional support system as being the equivalent of smoking 15 cigarettes a day. I had been single for around four years. That was 21,900 cigarettes. Or 21,915 if you include the leap year.

I realized I needed to get more serious about finding a life counterpart. I usually saw dating as laughable fun and games, figuring it would organically work itself out someday. I exerted minimal effort. This time I decided to enhance my dating potential with my new goals in mind. No more pursuing women just for fun. No more one-night stands. No more lies about playing professional hockey to get laid. And no more sex parties! Unless of course Bob thinks it will be, like, a really good one. So only really good sex parties. With good Champagne. Not André Brut.

I went back to Google and started looking into the St. Louis dating scene. It was a very vague search. I read about places to meet people, single person activities, support groups, and eventually something I had always mocked caught my eye in an intriguing manner. Within minutes, I had my credit card out and was signed up—that Thursday night I was attending a speed dating event.

34

Thursday night arrived and I stood in front of my wardrobe closet for what felt like half an hour. What should a guy wear to a speed dating event? A man's clothes say a lot about that person. I can tell when someone is going to be funny or interesting or an asshole before they open their mouths based on what they're wearing. Funny people don't give a rat's ass about their style. I can tell when someone is going to talk to me about sports. I can tell when someone is going to talk to me about Trump. I can tell when a man is going to hit on me. All based on their attire. I thought about how I wanted to come across to these potential girlfriends. Am I nonchalant and don't need to try hard? Basic black T-shirt and jeans kind of guy? The fact I was having this conversation in my head was proof enough that I was trying too hard. Maybe a nice button-up collared shirt, untucked with the sleeves rolled to imply it's time to get dirty and do some work, but I don't want to ruin my cuffs. Or how about a nice crisp white T-shirt under a dark blue knit cardigan sweater along with my speckled brown and black horn-rimmed glasses to show them how intellectual I am? Or maybe a full suit? Hey, look at how I overcame my crippling wealth to be here tonight. I have money. I will share it with you. I eventually went with a black tee and a basic mesh H&M jacket with extra pockets in places that made it seem the jacket was designed for a Tyrannosaurus Rex. I matched it with dark gray Levis and pointed-toe brown boots. Stylish but rugged. I nailed it once again.

When I arrived, I was surprised by the appearance of the women. I was expecting bovine-looking ladies. I'm sure they expected the same of the men. And they were right. Most of the guys were hideous. But these women were pleasing, aesthetically speaking. As we gathered in the lobby of the new Hotel St. Louis, everyone began to eye each other up, selecting hopeful favorites in their head, until a DJ started screaming into the microphone at everyone that we were about to get started. I wanted to ask him why the volume was so high. We were 15 feet away from him. I felt concerned for the guests of the hotel in rooms up to at least the fifth floor. Each female participant had a number with a corresponding numbered table. They were to remain stationary as the guys were to rotate tables every five minutes at the sound of the DJ's deafening claxon. I began mentally preparing myself for the event.

I convinced myself I needed to take it seriously. This was my most glaring problem in life. I was sick of being single and always chasing women. I needed to refrain from making constant jokes and sayings things of a weird nature. Half of my diction in life was usually said just to amuse myself or garner a response, like I was studying and experimenting with my own brain and the reactions of others. It was fair to assume this type of self-destruction was a central reason for my desolation. So for the event I thought, be funny but not Jim Carey funny. Not outlandish humor. Women don't want to sleep with Jim Carey, do they? His girlfriends have been attractive... no. Not Jim Carey funny. Be witty but be serious at times. Earnest. Drop the dry humor thing. Be normal. Okay, the DJ is screaming again...

After allowing everyone to check-in and get a drink, the nutbag on the mic instructed all the women to go to their tables. From there all the men were instructed to go to their numbered tables for their five-minute appointment, moving in numerical order after the time was up. It sounded impossible to mess up, yet some of the men were confused. Competition was obviously stiff.

The event began and it took all of two minutes before my attempt to refrain from dark and infantile humor failed. I could tell instantly that I wasn't interested in a woman in the time it took me to sit down in front of her. If that disinterest occurred, my objective switched directly into amusing myself. Here are some excerpts of conversations had:

Woman #8: What's the craziest thing you've done in the last 12 months?

Me: I went to a sex party while on MDMA.

Woman #3: All right Chris, what is your worst habit?

Me: Well I have a history of angry outbursts, so probably that. Or depression.

Woman #11: What do you look for in a woman?
Me: Hygiene.
Woman #11: Umm okay... anything else?
Me: Tolerance.
Woman #11: ...
Me: And I want a woman who holds in all her farts.

Even when I'm not around. I'll be able to tell.

Woman #11: I don't want to chat with you anymore.

Woman #4: So what's your biggest pet peeve?

Me: When my sister squeezes from the middle of our Preparation H tube and not the bottom. Also when my sister takes up the whole mattress. She is so annoying.

Woman #18: What's your idea of an ideal first date?

Me: Wine... great food...

Woman #18: (smiling)

Me: heavy petting... silence...

Woman #18 (not smiling)

Me: and maybe a movie, I don't know.

Me: Have you ever heard of a car accident fetish?

Woman #21: No...

Me: Excellent.

Woman #5: I like funny guys... tell me your favorite joke.

Me: Are you sure? Okay, umm... oh I got one! What's the difference between a joke and three hard dicks?

Woman #5: ...

Me: You don't look like you can take a joke! Ha ha.

Woman #16: So what do you think the most important thing in a relationship is?

Me: Good communication, for sure... and for her to stay away from the shed in the backyard.

Woman #13: Who was your first celebrity crush?

Me: The drummer from Hanson. I thought he was a

girl until I was like, 16.

Woman #1: Are you a morning or night person?

Me: Oh wow, a question with two possible one-word answers. I don't know, give me a few minutes to gather my thoughts.

Woman #2: Do you have any children?

Me: Who knows. I change my phone number a lot.

Woman #2: Are you joking?

Me: (not listening) There was that one kid who kept writing letters though.

Woman #19: What do you do for work?

Me: Have you ever heard of a fluffer?

Most of the women I met who were somewhat desirable, I derailed any chance of a possible phone number or date with my imbecilic jokes. All the other participants were about as appealing as poisonous mushrooms. One girl listed all her ex boyfriends chronologically, describing each one in depth. One girl I started to scream at because she said she didn't think Conan O'Brien was funny. I went on a rant about the comedic nuances and sheer brilliance of his writing and jokes, and then proceeded to call her a moron for not getting it. That was at about a minute and a half into the date, so we sat in silence drinking for the last three minutes. One spoke about the progress she was making with her therapist. One looked to be in her late-forties, despite the 35-year-old age cutoff. I didn't mind her at first. She seemed wise and well-traveled like my Aunt Linda. Which is what I said to her. She didn't think it was complimentary. One smelled like she just got out of a farting contest that went into overtime. One excused herself to go to the bathroom during our five minutes.

However, there was one girl—the last 'date' of the night—that aroused a strong connection. Fiona. She laughed at my dry sarcasm and was interesting. She was a 25-year-old country singer-songwriter waiting tables on the side to help finance her music aspirations. She had only come that night as support for her gross friend that told me I was unfunny. We had a great conversation, getting to know each other as well as two people could in a five-minute span. She agreed to go out with me. Everything about this girl seemed perfect. Until just before our session ended, she dropped the caveat. She was a born-again virgin.

35

I had never actually detested people that abstained from sex before marriage. Unless by 'detest' I mean I think it's fucking stupid. I had always thought it was fucking stupid. But they are someone else's stupid beliefs, not mine, so I'd never let it bother me. What had bothered me was the term 'born-again virgin'. You were not born again. You did not resurrect from the dead. And you're not a virgin. It was such a bullshit term for oneself. If you've had sex, there is nothing virginal about you. Can you be an anal virgin? Absolutely. Can you be a born-again virgin? Not if you have had sex. But I digress.

It was a blow to the balls, only figuratively at this point in the story, but it was certainly not a deal breaker. I liked sex. Sex was fun. At least for me it usually was. But it wasn't like I was having it with breakfast, lunch, and dinner like Ric Flair. I went 18 years (late bloomer) without it, so what's another three or four before I find and marry my soulmate? This was how my brain worked sometimes when I liked a girl. I wanted to be with her so bad I would completely block out and deny any glaring reasons why it would or would not work out. I could find out a girl had a devout posthumous faith to the workings of Hitler and if I liked her enough, I would let it slide.

Yeah she has a shrine to Hitler in her bedroom and a Swastika embroidered on her quilt, but she's not a bad person! She opened that door for that old lady carrying groceries once. And she's really hot.

So I decided to ignore the sexless factor and began dating Fiona. She was fun. Not necessarily good for my health however, as she usually worked Friday and Saturday nights either playing shows or waiting tables, so she always wanted to go out on Sunday and Monday nights. A typical industry gal. I could never wait until Sunday to drink so I usually kept my normal weekend booze schedule, either with friends or at her shows. She also played at an Irish bar every Thursday night that I frequented. This resulted in several four or five-day benders. But we made it work. Date nights twice a week, usually a night in together. We kept things interesting and fun; everything was going steady for a while... until I met her family.

36

The first meeting with Fiona's parents was a very impromptu one. They had a dinner planned for her older sister's very recent engagement to her long-term boyfriend. Apparently Fiona informed me of the dinner a week prior and I was not paying attention. Saturday came and I treated it as any other Saturday in our relationship—she was working and I had free reign to get drunk with my friends. I found myself at a bar in Soulard just before 1:00 pm. My friend Jesse and I cruised the neighborhood on his golf cart, visiting seven or eight bars in a four-hour span before I received the dreaded text from Fiona at 5:07 pm.

Hey just be at my parents' house by 6:30. Here's the address

My drunk brain's first thought was that she must have texted the wrong person, messaging me accidentally instead of her friend. But I received no follow up, so I texted back.

Parrdonnn?

Incoming Call: Fiona

The phone call was a buzz kill to say the least. She was very upset and didn't laugh at any of my jokes. She instructed me to go home, shower, sober up, and get the fuck over to her parents' house. I said I could not drive.

She said get a fucking Uber. I asked her what's with the rude language. She swore again and hung up.

I arrived at Fiona's parents' house without having a drink for the previous hour or so. This made first greetings go okay, but I was still very drunk. I was concealing it tactfully until her mom offered me a glass of wine.

"No, he's fine," Fiona blurted out.

"Yes pleeeaaassse," I said. Her mom squinted at me and poured me a glass. After lounging in the living room for a bit, avoiding any real conversation, the table was set for dinner and we took our seats. Conversation ensued.

"So Chris, Fiona says you work in advertising? What's that like?" her mom asked. I was not paying attention. Silence permeated the room for several seconds.

"Chris?" Fiona commanded. "My mom asked you a question."

"Sorry, what? Can you be more specific?" I said with glassy eyes.

"Like what do you do each day at work?" Fiona was sitting next to her as nervous as I'd ever seen her, shooting me perpetual stink-eyes.

"Basically I try to deceive the public. The key is to be as unethical as possible without breaking any rules of the FCC or Advertising Standards Authority. I am pretty decent at it. I think that's how I got Fiona to go out with me actually."

Luckily everyone at the table laughed. Everyone except Fiona. Getting one laugh was all it took for me to start being more charming than off-putting, and the dinner was going well despite Fiona wanting to stab me with a carving knife the entire time. Her dad remained silent, but her mom continued to pepper me with questions. I was destroying them one by one like a ¢50 game of Asteroids.

"Is work anything like that show *Mad Men*? I love that show!"

"Kind of. The socialization aspect of it is accurate. We basically just stand around and drink whiskey most days. We are nicer to the receptionists behind their backs though." Even her dad laughed at that remark. I decided I wanted more wine and helped myself to another glass. Fiona kicked me underneath the table.

"Ouch!" I dramatically yelped.

"Oh, what's wrong dear?" her mom asked.

"Cramp," I winced.

I ignored Fiona's physical censure to my wine pouring and topped it even higher in the glass and winked at her. Two concurrent mistakes.

As I became more inebriated, I started to lose my barometer for charm and humor and started to say rude things accidentally. I took my new comfort level too far.

"So, working on any fun projects at the moment Chris?" her mom asked from the kitchen.

"Goddammit, Barb! All you do is talk about work. What's for dinner?! Ha ha ha!"

"Chris!" Fiona whispered at me in a chastising tone.

"Smells pretty good, Barb!" I yelled, trying to recover.

The food did not help because I was not hungry. I barely ate and it became noticeable I was drunk midway through the meal. At one point, looking around their dining room and living room in the distance I noticed a lot of Catholic decor and decided to comment on it.

"Wow, you guys sure love that Jesus guy, eh? I've heard good things. His hair was cool."

The rest of the dinner was hazy but Fiona made it

clear it did not go well. She drove me home in silence. She didn't talk to me for a full three days after that.

37

If you thought overcoming a fight with your significant other was difficult enough, try doing it without make-up sex. It was a grim week, but we managed to overcome my brilliant performance at her parents' house. We continued dating. Which also meant we continued not having sex. I always thought blue balls was a myth. Just jerk off, job done. But blue balls were a very real thing. So much so that mine were more of an ebony or a midnight black. Onyx, almost. Whatever color outer space is, that is what type of colored balls I had after four months of dating Fiona. They felt like an active volcano that could erupt at any minute. I didn't know if sex would elicit a river of cum or a puff of smoke at that point. I then started to think about her privates. The inside of her vagina must have looked like the top of an unused ceiling fan. When she said she was abstaining from sex she meant everything. Hand jobs were a sin. Blowjobs were the devil's work. The disciples warranted dry-humping however. Dry-humping soon became my least favorite activity. It was torture. I felt like a cat chasing a laser pointer around the room. I was too stupid to realize I would never catch it, but hope remained.

After about another month of dating my issues with

the lack of sex stagnated. My penis gave up and became complacent. That sounds sad, but it made me happy. I was fortunate to be with Fiona and while our schedules still did not coordinate well, I was enjoying our relationship. I felt hypnotized. A lifeless boyfriend zombie in a half-conscious stupor. I enjoyed using the phrase 'my girlfriend'. I talked about her frequently like she was a current event. I even went to church with her once. I didn't know if I was in love with her, but for the first time in years I had a woman I was happy to be with long-term. But this comfort level soon turned into my demise. I stopped trying to impress her. My complacency quickly turned against me as she started to notice *my* flaws manifest before her eyes and the excitement of a new relationship passed. I noticed her lack of enthusiasm in our relationship. She canceled dates. Her texts were shorter. She blanked my phone calls and then texted me back instead. I decided to ignore these indicators for a few days and stopped reaching out. Three days went by without communication from either side until a lengthy text from her pinged.

She had broken up with me.

Karma.

38

Getting dumped from the first relationship I had in years after only five months had an unspeakable misery to it. The long-winded text she taped out was sent while she was on a break at work. I called repeatedly. Texted multiple times, only to get back in response, *I'm at work I'm sorry.* That night I didn't sleep. I sat on my couch watching Netflix for six hours straight, trying to escape my thoughts. I called in sick the next day at work. I walked around downtown for hours thinking about her and what was wrong with me. I should have been thrilled I could have sex again, humping the nearest willing, breathing female biped in sight, but I was weirdly depressed for a long while. I deserved it.

After a week of self-hatred and moping around, my life began to feel disheveled for what felt like different reasons. Reasons I couldn't quite figure out. It was just a holistic depression, not a feeling caused from Fiona or work or never getting a date with Jamie, just from my life in general. Maybe my time in St. Louis had expired. It festered in my mind for days on end. A lot of things happened in those following months that were out of character, insolent, and morbidly unhealthy.

For example I started taking my frustrations out at

work. That following week I had a new crêpe restaurant in town assigned to me as a client. In our initial meeting, unprepared and trying to improvise, I spent 45 minutes trying to convince them to name their restaurant Serial Crêpist. I told them it was a solvent name for the business with the current #MeToo media attention. The owner was so offended she and her business partners walked out of the meeting and fired our firm. I told her she would be out of business in six months.

At a Cardinals game on alcohol and narcotics, I saw Jamie—my avowed unicorn. That was the first time I had seen her since we met. She was sitting at a table in the bar area of the common space VIP lounge we were both in. I went up to her and before I could get halfway through a sentence, I spilt her drink in her lap. Also as it turned out it wasn't Jamie.

On one occasion I hit on one of my best friend's recent ex-girlfriend at a bar in front him, not able to distinguish her from all the other blonde girls in her group. He didn't speak to me for weeks.

Out at a friend's cabin at the lake, I got a blowjob from someone's mom or aunt in a vacant boathouse. Can't remember how it happened or whose family member it was. She wiped off my dick with an orange life jacket. I think her husband was in the cabin.

For three weeks I dated a 19-year-old with braces. She had no redeeming qualities other than she couldn't see me being unfaithful to her in bars due to her age. I didn't introduce her to anyone because I was ashamed of her metal braces.

And lastly, I got into a physical altercation with a Washington Avenue homeless guy. All because he wouldn't let me buy him a box of rice. I was partially drunk, walking by and he asked if I had a dollar because he was trying to buy a box of rice. At first I said no, but then became intrigued about the absurdity of his request and went up to him to inquire. "Why would you want a box of rice?"

"Man, I'm hungry."

"How the hell are you gonna cook it?"

"Don't worry about that, man."

"I am not worried. I'm just curious."

"You got a dollar or not?"

I had several dollars. I was convinced he, like most of the street mongrels, was just going to use whatever money he got to buy drugs or alcohol. A noble cause to be sure, just not on my dollar. They usually say they need money for a bus pass to get home. Classic lie. Or a sandwich. Wanting money for a sandwich is in the Bum Fibs Hall of Fame. If they were just honest with me and said they wanted to get drunk, I'd be much more inclined to give them money. I have bought too many drinks in bars for strangers to count over the years. I didn't see how it was much different. But those people were not lying and trying to swindle me. I became uncharacteristically irate at this homeless guy and told him I would take him to the store and buy him a box of rice to call his bluff. "Buddy," I said, "I will take you to the Culinaria right now and get you a box of rice if you really want it." The vagrant stood there for several seconds, looking at me like I had just asked him to get on my spaceship. Very confused. Finally he agreed, "All right man, let's go. Thanks."

It was obvious he wanted nothing to do with stale rice, especially with no discernible way of boiling it. So fucking absurd. I think at first he thought, Okay if I go with this dude he will get me a box of rice, but maybe I can get a tall boy out of it. I'll tell him I need something to wash it down with. We didn't even get 20 steps down the block before he stopped and aggressively said, "Man, FUCK THIS AND FUCK YOU," while turning around and started to walk back the other way.

This prick couldn't even pretend to be grateful for someone buying him food he didn't want. Like he didn't have 10 minutes in his fucking busy homeless schedule? I became even more irate and called him a piece of shit. He turned, squared up, and pushed me. I pushed him back harder, throwing him into a brick wall where he smashed the side of his head and fell to the ground. He started bleeding. He stumbled back to his feet and ran off.

Later that night, more inebriated, I nearly cried about the event. I was sitting on my couch, head in my hands, repeatedly calling myself a loser and an asshole while on the verge of tears. I was losing my mind.

39

It turned out I did in fact lose my mind. As well as my love for the city of St. Louis. Two weeks later I quit my job on a whim. I applied for and was granted a one-year travel visa to Australia. I bought a one-way ticket to Sydney. I sold nearly everything in my apartment. I called my mom and said I was coming home for a month before my flight. She was confused. I couldn't tell if the move was a brilliant idea or a terrible mistake brought on by depression and impulsiveness. Either way the ticket and my hostel fee for first week's stay was non-refundable. I only said a handful of goodbyes in St. Louis. Most people I simply withdrew from conversation with, depriving them of an explanation. Greg took the news with indifference. He just shook my hand and said, "What twisted webs we weave, eh? Good luck, Christopher." I told David personally as well. He cried on my shoulder for several minutes. The most difficult goodbye was probably the sous chef at Tani Sushi. As a long-term diner that was very emotional for me, probably not so much for him. He actually seemed confused. I'm not sure he spoke English. I told Miles, Jim, and Daryl and Daryl responded with, "Oh man, we gotta pick a weekend to come out there." I do not think he was aware of the 20-hour flight, but I appreciated the sentiment. I tried to tell Bob but he was on a 90-day bender in Southeast Asia with no cell phone.

I chose Australia because its alcohol prices were among the highest in the world. Because of my strict frugality, that meant I would not drink as often as I wanted to. I also chose Australia because it was an English-speaking country with beautiful women and beaches. Sitting in the airport a month later waiting for my departure, I contemplated the future and what was to come. I had no responsibilities, nobody to answer to. For the first time in years I didn't care that I was single. I was happy about it.

As I took my seat on the flight, I thought about Jamie, and I realized that I never did see her again. I had yet to meet a girl I was intrigued by as much as her since we last spoke. Not even Fiona, my ex, who I purposefully withheld a goodbye to. Minutes away from flying across the world to a foreign country where I would obtain a new foreign phone number, I decided to text Jamie one last time out of curiosity. It had been over half a year since she ghosted me. I formed the text as simple as possible, with no resentment.

Hey Jamie, it's Chris. Still have any interest in going out sometime?

She responded immediately.

Oh my God, hi Chris! Yes I would love to. Are you free tomorrow night?

Dating in a nutshell.

ABOUT THE AUTHOR

@homeferdinner

Michael Dennis was born in St. Paul, Minnesota in 1989. He grew up in Superior, Wisconsin and transplanted to St. Louis, Missouri in 2013 where he unfortunately, still resides. *Single and Loathing It* is his debut novel.

ACKNOWLEDGMENTS

The author is pleased to express grateful acknowledgment and appreciation to friend and editor Ben Way. He also wishes to acknowledge the following who read raw and unedited first draft ramblings and offered valuable feedback: Mitch, Tim, JP, Taylor, Anthony, Randy, Amar, Bob, Tron, Piper, YP, Packy, Paul, and Katie even though she admitted she was always too high to get through the first page. Also sorry Brenden, the author forgot to send. And thanks to Austin for hilarious conversations and ideas.

CPSIA information can be obtained
at www.ICGtesting.com
Printed in the USA
LVHW090031151119
637441LV00001B/156/P